Looking Back....
Knowing that you gave it
Your very all....
Win or Lose
You finish a champion -
"THE SPIRIT"
-30-
Dale Earnhardt

SPIRIT

YOU KNOW ABOUT NASCAR AND THE
BIG RACING ORGANIZATIONS ...

YOU KNOW ABOUT THE FANTASTIC
200 MPH DRIVERS...

NOW IT IS TIME...

NOW IT IS TIME THAT YOU KNOW
HOW IT ALL BEGAN...

NOW IT IS TIME FOR...

THE SPIRIT
by
Johnny Frederick

MEET THE ELECTRIFIING CHARACTER
KNOWN ONLY AS "SPOOK" PERHAPS THE
GREATEST DRIVER IN THE WORLD...

FROM THE SINGING SISES...TO THE DETROIT
SUPERCARS...HE WAS MASTER OF THEM ALL...

COMING IN EARLY SUMMER AT
MOST BOOK STORES...

The Spirit

by

JOHNNY FREDERICK

authorHOUSE®

AuthorHouse™
1663 Liberty Drive
Bloomington, IN 47403
www.authorhouse.com
Phone: 1-800-839-8640

First published by AuthorHouse 05/31/2011

ISBN: 978-1-4490-5969-9 (sc)
ISBN: 978-1-4490-5970-5 (dj)
ISBN: 978-1-4490-5971-2 (e)

Printed in the United States of America

Photos in this book by Author

Any people depicted in stock imagery provided by Thinkstock are models, and such images are being used for illustrative purposes only. Certain stock imagery © Thinkstock.

This book is printed on acid-free paper.

To the memory of
Bobby Isaac
And
To All Those Who within Their Hearts,
Beats The Spirit Of A Racer...
And To Valerie,
"With The Gentlest Heart of All"

MAIN CHARACTERS

Spook: the greatest driver in the world. Who thought he knew what the end was to be.

Mary Jacobs: Loved the Spook but couldn't understand him until too late.

Rudy Lock: Veteran driver, fierce opponent of the Spook on the track...and where Miss Mary was concerned.

Doc Toner: Anyone can make a mistake.

Bill Nordic: Auto dealer. Could see what was happening but was helpless to stop it.

MISC CHARACTERS:

Jerry Adams, Buck Peter, Pat Jensen. Team drivers for Nordic and Clark Motors.

The years of brooking and self-pity had taken their inevitable toll on Doc Toner's mind, and his irrational thinking, agitated by the blaspheming engines from the speedway made itself plain in his ranting speech:

"I hear you, you treacherous demons. Scream all you like, for I'll put an end to you before long." He shook a crooked finger in the direction of the track.

The large envelope lay on his desk untouched, through plainly marked: Urgent! Leave it lay, Doc thought. He knew the contents of it anyway, so why bother to open it. He rose from his chair and walked to the window, peering out at the speedway several blocks down the street. Dark exhaust smoke hung over the track and it was this that Doc found cause to begin ranting again.

"Look there… look at it…it's the smoke of hell… that's what it is!" He flung a hand before his eyes and rushed back to his desk, where he buried his face in his hands and wept for "the boys."

With a sudden whim of his sick mind, he tore open the large envelope, and unfolded the enclosed letter with shaking hands. It read:

"Upon examining the blood sample sent us by your office, we find no cause for alarm. True, a blood deficiency is evident, but certainly not a cancerous condition.

What is now the nature of your patient's activities and has that person been informed of a cancerous blood malady? If so, please advise said person, as the psychological effects could be damaging. Advise our office, immediately."

Doc dropped the letter as if it were a heated coal, the shocking contents of its white interior bringing back normal senses. He burst from the office and ran like a person possessed for the tumultuous strife of the speedway!

The pace he was setting couldn't last. If he continued at the speed the car would blow up, if it wasn't disintegrated in one of the turns first. If he had still been on our team, I would have had Pat Polotel flag him in, but as it was, I had no say. I felt that if it hadn't have been the last race of the season, the Association officials would have flagged him in.

In the midst of this fascinating yet fearful thing, Doc Toner, his eyes wild and bloodshot, rushed up to me; "Bill, Bill, you've got to stop this race!" His breath came in short, rasping gulps, like he had been running, and he leaned on one of the cars for support.

"What the hell are you doing here, Doc? I thought you didn't..."

He cut me off. "Bill, you've got to stop the Spook...now... hurry!" he shook me by my shirt front.

"What's the matter with you, Doc...I can't stop him...he's racing."

"I know...I know he's racing...listen...listen to me, please. He came to me for medical attention...and I made a mistake...I told him...I told him he had leukemia...but he hasn't, Bill he hasn't!"

"Good God, Doc, then that's why...!" I ran over to Mary and slapped her out of her trance. She sobbed and struck at me.

Marty screamed, "Bill, Bill...what are you doing?" I told them, in a panic-stricken voice what was happening, then tripped and stumbled, with legs gone numb, for the flag man! I had to stop the race before...The crowd roared in terror at the number 30 car, out of control!

Doc Toner stood there, the figure of a beaten man. He had made another mistake and one of "the boys" was in serious danger because of him and his erroneous calculations. He watched with tear-blurred eyes as Bill Nordic fought his way through the litter filled pits, and gasped as he saw Nordic halt and shake a young girl, who began striking at him.

THE SPIRIT
By Johnny Frederick, 1956

He had another name, but in the several years that I knew him and was associated with him I never heard it mentioned. Oh, it was down on his business papers and things like that, but always he was referred to as the Spook. I first saw him on a clear, summer day in June 1950, at the time my partner, Tom Clark, and I had three competition cars entered with Tri-State Stock Car Association (T.S.S.C.A.)

The Spook, who must have been around twenty-five then, was leaning against a concession stand watching the cars whip through the asphalt circle in a practice session at our local Norfolk speedway.

I don't know what it was that made him catch my eye, unless it was the way which he watched the stockers streak down the straights and brake frantically for the turns. There seemed to be no emotion whatsoever on his chalky countenance as a Ford spun out in the path of one of our Hudsons!

There was a tearing crash as the two racers slammed together, the Ford spinning and swapping ends three times before at last coming to a teetering rest!

The lean, somber-faced youth only shifted his weight, a slight, secret smile appearing momentarily at the corners of his mouth.

Our number 20, with Pat Jensen as pilot, was forced steaming from the track, his front end smashed.

I started over to the pit area then, only to be taken back by the changed expression on the Spook's face. The eyes were a terrible thing, piercing, bottomless voids nearly beyond description.

The skin was drawn tight over his high cheekbones and was of a deathly, almost mild white pallor. Upon passing by him, I could actually feel the drive of a boundless, pent-in energy, crying for an escape!

A sense of urgency was about me, warning me to get away from that youth with the destitute eyes and overwhelming sinister air about him. His whole being suggested a soul afire with an uncontrollable, driving force. I hastened my pace even more, not glancing back until I had reached the familiarity of the pits and then it was only to find him gone.

Shaking my head in puzzlement, I flipped up my coat collar at the sudden, chill wind that seemed to be coming from the direction of the concession stand.

The season had gone well for us down at Nordic and Clark, Hudson Dealers, with the Hudson doing extremely well all over the country. The Tri-State season had begun only that Easter Sunday with a 200-miler at our Norfolk speedway and our Hudsons finished with the top five cars. Our keenest competitors were the factory backed teams of Plymouth and Olds. We had not received any aid from the Hudson factory in past years, but with the advent of our factory participation, were promised assistance early in the conflict of the 1950 circuit. Factory sponsorship was steadily increasing and it was feared by many that the day may soon come when the independent entry, the backbone of stock car racing, would no longer be able to compete against the limitless funds and expendable cars of the big factory organizations. Tom Clark and I had discussed the matter only the previous day. Yes, the writing was on the wall for all to see. The Detroit Barons wanted to dominate the racing scene, mostly because of the tremendous publicity potential it could represent for their eager sales departments.

The accent was, even then, on higher performance engines, faster accelerating cars. The cars were improving, too, as far as top speed and stop light dig were concerned, but unfortunately, the most important factor of a high performance machine was forgotten, or at least had to wait its turn. The stockers were beginning to go like real bombs, but the handling characteristics left something to be desired, especially in the weight distribution picture.

That's why we at the various Hudson dealerships felt we had a superior car. Nothing on the circuit could handle with our cars and what we did lack in acceleration compared to the Olds Rocket, we more than made up by getting through the turns faster. If the stockers were to become even swifter, as rumored, the uncalled for weight distribution of a blackjack would have to be remedied. Perhaps, too, that was the reason the big boys from Detroit were delving into the game. People began to wonder about a particular car when they saw six entries of that make on the track, five of which went out of the contest very early with one common ailment. Yes, Detroit was wise to investigate the circuit, the real proving ground for their labors!

Since the initiation of the Tri-State organization in 1948, large purses were offered by track managers and businessmen alike, to encourage drivers to compete. If a man were skilled enough and possessed that rare temperament necessary for a successful racer, he may well finish a season several thousand dollars ahead, particularly, if he were driving for one of the teams.

Pat Jensen, Jerry Adams and Buck Peters of our team were doing remarkably well in the short time they had driven. Buck a former bus driver in one of the major southern cities, was a splendid driver and on occasions had outmaneuvered the swaggering Rudy Lock of the Olds team. He had no difficulty in adapting himself to the slam-bang of racing and we were most fortunate to have a driver of his caliber on our team.

Jerry Adams was a planning, calculative driver who never took an unnecessary risk. His keen, sharp judgment had more than once netted us finishes within the top ten. Rather on the short side, Jerry appeared dwarfed when standing alongside Buck's towering frame. An interesting feature of Jerry's was his quick smile that somehow formed on only half his face. Often times the boys affectionately referred to him as "Jock-strap Jerry with his lopsided grin."

Pat Jensen, at thirty-five, was the oldest member in the driving realm. A good, solid and dependable pilot, Pat was also quite handy when it came to repairs and welding. A northwest boy, he always threatening to return to the cool, moist forests of his home state whenever the merciless sun was exceptionally hot. I had always felt that Pat would as soon be working on the cars as guiding them down the blistering asphalt, but he never requested a job in the shop so we kept him on the cars. Possibly, he wanted the opportunity to win the ever growing purses, or the track may have gotten so far into his system that it was impossible for him to break away. At any rate, we had a splendid performer in Pat and would always welcome his serious, contemplating face in whatever mischief we might be about.

— — — — — — — — — — — —

Jacking up the right front wheel of the red Plymouth the Spook began changing operations. The tire may go another lap, or again it may not. A driver who had to overcome the ever increasing number of factory entries couldn't afford to lose a tire during the churning heat of a contest, possibly losing his one and only car by ramming the fence, or worse, into the path of an aggressive factory car.

He had arrived here in Norfolk last Thursday and had trial ran the 97 horsepower Plymouth over the track, getting the feel of it. A good track, a fast track, that would leave the Plymouth somewhat at a loss to the swifter cars.

But the durable power plant and general dependability of the whole car was not to be easily dismissed, as he had proved to many hot drivers on the West Coast, where he had formerly raced. Here in Norfolk, the attractive prizes were drawing the competitive breed from all corners and circles where racing was prevalent. Few possessed the skill of the Spook when it came to "setting up" a car for the track, and fewer still had his uncanny understanding of hurtling through a run, flat out, full bore! The man and the machine were one, both on and off the track. The "magic hands" tuned the sewing machine engine to perfection, drawing out every bit of its screeching voice of power. The car's rigid suspension and "beefed up" drive train were in a class all their own, when made ready by the strange, icy individual known only as the Spook. Here was a car that would handle with the Hudsons and run the Olds ragged with its ceaseless, thriving power.

The Spook, who was a racer by nature, lived for the hazards and uncertainty of the circuit. To be absent from the business of risk and chance for even a short length of time tore at his very heart, his every fiber crying for crescendo of a high revving engine. Thus it was that he looked forward to the coming battle of the Tri-State circuit, said to be the fiercest in the land!

Doc Toner sat hunched over in his small, dusty office. At sixty-five, Doc was somewhat bitter against the tiring struggle called life. Here, far removed from the big city hospitals, a skillful surgeon whiled away his life in meaningless existence, delivering an occasional child, patching up a careless hunter, or simply giving his advice to those seeking his opinion. He had been asked for his opinion once before, so many years ago, and those concerned had followed that advice.

He had been a young, struggling intern then, aglow with the thought of making sick people well, casting out prejudices and above all, assisting the young. He loved youth and its lightheartedness, for he too had been young then. He sadly shook his graying head from side to side, the many wrinkles on his heavy brow deep and lending an air of self-pity to the man himself.

How had he known that his few words, spoken in the haste of a rush-rush schedule, were to end the life of an emergency case? The others, they hadn't known what to do...would not the frail woman have succumbed no matter what they had done to try and save her?

A hospital full of interns and student nurses on a Sunday afternoon such a long time ago, and that had been the conclusion of his ambitious career...Any human could have made the error, even Doctor Vogelman had told him that. But remembering the sight of that poor woman, writhing in agony, had been too much for Doc and he had thrown away the whole thing, the hours of study and hardship, the sacrifices his old father had made to see him, some day, a brilliant surgeon. Had not the whole staff voted him the most promising of all the new interns, going out of their way often times to help him further his ever-growing knowledge? Had he let them down in any way? That was Doc's concern, or at least had been at first. Now, he just didn't care much, what with his own youth gone and his will for life itself, a makes-no-difference affair. The time was past for action now, so he just didn't worry about it anymore. His chest was heavy, sometimes aching, and he was tired to his very soul; He just didn't care.

He had watched this thing grow over the past few years…this senseless business called racing and perhaps that's what was preying on his long stilled ambition and vitality, for racing involved those he dearly loved…the young. He cringed at the thought of "the boys" as he called them, risking their health, their very lives, guiding those charging pieces of iron and steel in a never ending circle. There had been young Toby, killed on the '49 circuit, and young Jack, whose laughter was like a bubbling stream, even before that. All these things Doc remembered sitting in the lonely emptiness of his cubby-hole office, and he was depressed even more. He prayed that the butchery would soon cease, but was shocked to see the increasing number of racing cars, appearing for Sunday's event. Big cars, little cars, they all looked alike to Doc and he hated them down to their last nut and bolt.

The drivers themselves though, that was another story. There were "the boys" seeking thrills, finding them in the whining of a blasphemous engine. Blasphemous those hated engines must be, to draw the young to them, hypnotizing them with their false promise of adventure.

There were "the boys" who were in their late thirties, lulled into dreariness by those scheming creatures. Beginning with the old jalopies, the years slipping past, until they were no longer the kids full of eagerness that they had been. With nowhere to turn, they followed the engines from one race to the next. The sly beckoning of the engines had betrayed them, and they were confused, waiting for whatever was dealt them. Nary a whimper though, for "the boys" never cried.

Doc was infinitely correct, he felt. Maybe it was the loneliness of his own spirit that made him seek so deeply the motives of others.

The only "boys" that thoroughly escaped his comprehension were those very few. Those very few that lived only for the risks of the circuit. Boys, who laughed at death and its long-reaching, bony hand and spat in his face if he were close, They loved the misleading, banshee wail of those despised engines, with a passion usually reserved for a beautiful woman.

To take away their races and their cars would be to destroy their very reason for existence. What manner of boys were they? Could they be representatives of the evil one himself? Doc shuddered at the disturbing thought, a cold blast of wind engulfing his small shoulders, as he looked through the window at a red Plymouth with the number 30 on its glimmering side glide by.

Another one had arrived in town, he thought. This one with a face one would not easily forget. Doc rubbed his stubbled chin and was again blasted by an icy draft. Frowning, he rose, stumped stiffly over to close his office door…

The door was already closed…

— — — — — — — — — — —

Assembling my drivers together, as was always my practice prior to a contest, I impressed the fact on the drivers, that with the large field that was developing, our chances for the top three spots were rapidly declining. The hateful Rudy Lock, from over Polson way, was present with the Olds team, yelling and griping at his pit crew, who were doing their utmost in last minute preparation on his yellow number 61 Rocket. He was a driver to be reckoned with on any track, having gained the most points last season of any driver on the Tri-State circuit.

To hear Rudy tell it, Miss Mary Jacobs, queen of the race that Sunday, was strictly his girl. Always, openly boasting of his skill with the ladies, stating he could steal the heart of a broad as easily as he could defeat Nordic's Hudsons on the track. He would get a big charge out of his wittiness, laughing and carrying on like a nit-wit, his whiskey-reddened features taking on a purplish tinge with every note of boisterous laughter.

Removed from the track, he was a bar room tough, with a big reputation for bulliness. Don't misunderstand me. Rudy was no coward and would tackle a rhino if egged on, but he much preferred s sure thing, often insulting young guys out with their dates, then clobbering the smaller men in front of their girls. This unruly type of thing was his specialty. I guess it has done something for his twisted ego, or exulted his already high opinion of himself. Unfortunately as a competitor on the stock car tracks, he was much the same, slamming his opponents at each and every opportunity.

Before the factories dealt themselves a hand in our racing program and Rudy was an independent, we had kept his unsportsmanlike tactics under control, threatening the big man with license termination.

With Detroit on the scene, many of our old rules were difficult to enforce because their drivers, too, were somewhat rowdy. Whenever Bob French, of headquarters, complained or penalized any offenders, the manufacturers gave him a rough time. Yes, the old jalopies that we used to have so much fun with on a Sunday afternoon, had disappeared, and in their place was a highbred machine that was constantly improving.

I think that all the true racing advocates longed for the past ways of doing things. It was becoming mighty hot for an independent entry to even place in a race and it seemed that factory backing was a must. I was relieved when our first check arrived from Hudson. On the face of that check, it had read "Payable to Nordic and Clark Motors – Racing Division." Get that . . . racing division! Something new had been added, bitter oaths filling the pit area, as one team manager cursed another. Our circuit was turning into a harsh, heartless nightmare.

I never understood what it was the charming Miss Mary saw in Rudy lock. True, he could be gracious at times, but was definitely pretty crude on the whole. Some of his worse vices had disappeared since he began dating Mary and I was reasonably sure that he was stuck on her.

Miss Mary and I were no strangers and she had often confided in my wife Marty and me during her school years. Now, nearly twenty-one, she had grown into a bewitching young woman. Standing tall and shapely, many a lustful glance was cast her way. A vibrant personality, slightly hidden shell of reserve, serious-minded to the extent of being plagued by the blues on numerous occasions, at which time Marty and I always had an encouraging word for her.

I suppose one could surmise that was the reason she went with Rudy, him being such an extrovert and all.

I sincerely hoped that Mary wouldn't fall for the man. The most striking characteristic about Mary were her eyes. Such lovely eyes, full of expression and life. Green, glowing emeralds that could melt the harshest of men, with only a soft glance. I found myself comparing her eyes to those terrible and dangerous ones that I had seen on the slender, white-faced youth, earlier in the day.

Saturday afternoon I wolfed down a quick lunch, kissed Mart

goodbye, and headed for the shop. I was anxious to see how the cars were progressing in readiness for the 250-miler, scheduled at our speedway for Sunday afternoon. Out of state cars and drivers had been drifting into town all week, the potent Olds team from Polson among them. Rudy's 61 car was parked in front of Mary's place on Cartwright Street. Other factory Olds lined the curb in front of Nick Sitell's Exhaust Note, plush gathering place of nearly all the drivers.

As I entered the shop Tom came over and slipped his arm over my shoulder pointing at Elmer, our key mechanic. Elmer had his head buried under the hood of one of the Hudson's, the engines turning up at around 3,000, being checked for cut out. Elmer was a bird all his own, never saying a word, often times even when asked. He labored on the cars with indefatigable endurance, his lips puckered, his head cocked sideways when engrossed with some difficult to find ignition miss or carburetor slopover. We always got a big charge out of watching him when he was puzzled, Tom usually laughing aloud in amusement. We were fortunate to have Elmer, George, his able assistant, and the other skillful members that made up our pit crew. I informed Tom that I already had spoken to the drivers about the ever growing number of entries and he agreed that it would be a tough show all the way through.

The impersonal voice of the loud speaker announced the cars participating in the event, as the stockers received last moment plug installations, tire changes and hasty check overs by the excited pitmen. Miss Mary, surrounded by her royal court, had taken her place in the queen's box waving to Rudy as he sped over the asphalt in practice laps. Pat put our number 20 around the circle with very impressive lap times and was soon dueling it out with

Rudy Lock in the back stretch. The Hudson walked right down the straight with the bellowing Rocket, but Pat pulled into the pits on the completion of that same lap. I had always instructed my drivers not to engage individual contestants prior to the official race itself. The conceited Rudy, of course, thought Pat was afraid to be on the track alone with him and made a big spectacle of himself in front of Miss Mary. He would accelerate down the straights, brake furiously for the corners, power through them, the oversized tires on the Olds screaming in protest, then blast again down the straight to repeat the same procedure, Mary cheering him on.

It was that first race where the bitter rivalry started between Rudy and the Spook, though I don't think the Spook was aware of the reason for Rudy's animosity at the time. I saw the red Plymouth pull onto the track, but didn't know the car from any former events. It was only when the number 30 swept by out pit that I recognized the pale youth. I remember how taken back I had felt upon suddenly seeing him there on the track, the name "Spook" painted in bold white lettering above the door.

He held the little Plymouth to the extreme right of the track as Rudy roared past once more. He stomped on the throttle then, surging ahead with liquid smooth shifts, within one lap fastening himself on the bumper of the wildly driven Olds: Rudy threw the Olds into the south turn, but the Plymouth was still reflecting its bright color back at him in his mirror as he power slid out of the turn. He charged ahead of the Plymouth by several lengths on the straight, only to find himself staring into the north turn. Braking savagely down, he once again had a mirror full of determined Plymouth. At the point of adhesion, the Spook bumped the Olds causing the rear end to break loose. He then sped by

18

the flabbergasted Rudy on the inside, shooting down the straight in the lead. Rudy, crossways on the track did a splendid job of recovering the Rocket from a near spin out, and set out on the vengeance trail. His revenge would have to wait, or so it seemed, as he found himself unable to match the lap times of the intruder in the fire red car.

The Spook wouldn't slack off two cents worth, but went flat out through the turns while Rudy, thinking he could put the Olds through the same test, found that the big, heavy nosed brute would break away, the whole car shaking in protest.

He tried again on the next straight, blasting out of the north turn six lengths behind the Plymouth. He was right on the little red fanny for the south corner, but had to brake once more, the Plymouth scuttling away.

The crowd was cheering with delight, as the contesting duo continued, until the Rocket's brakes began smoking rather badly. While the Spook kept circling, Rudy sped into the pits, grabbing a team-mate's car.

Accelerating ahead of the Spook, he once more held to the inside of the track. It didn't make any difference to that dead-faced youngster in the screaming red machine. He only rode the Rocket hard into the turns again, and just when Rudy was preparing to be bumped, the Spook pulled around him on the right, slipping a bet, then skipping away. We all had a good laugh on that one. Apparently, this Spook was a very flexible driver, Rudy went frothing back to the Olds pit yelling and blowing at anyone who would listen, his face as red as the 30 car, and I'm sure his anger and humiliation were aimed solely at that bright car and its very uncommon driver.

The Spook was changing plugs when I walked up to him in

the independent pits. He looked paler than I had remembered him from the other day and believe me that's pretty pale. No sign of strain or anxiety showed on the cold features as he nodded to me. I said merrily, "that was a fine ride. It looks to me as if you may wind up with the coveted Queen's kiss" and gestured toward the royalty section. The terrible eyes fastened on Miss Mary, who had been observing him. Something was born at the moment their eyes met and a beautiful yet tragic feeling was in the air, if you can understand that. The glowing, green eyes of Mary softened and shone into the terrible fixed gaze of him, the Spook. The hollow face came alive and the terrible eyes subsided. There was little doubt in my mind as to who would be victorious that afternoon such a long time ago.

Smoke and gas fumes hovered over the pack of multicolored cars, the din of their combined engines making ones heart flutter and pound harder against the rib cage. Pete Nichols, speedway president, was driving the official pace car, the lovely Miss Mary seated beside him. The cars rolled around the track in disorder once, twice, faster the second time, taking up their positions. On the third circle, starter Pat Polotel gave them the green flag. The pace car dove for the cover of the pit area as the relentless racers shot past. Pat, the Spook, Rudy and Buck made up the first four places, in that order. They maintained those positions until the fiftieth lap, when the Spook made his bid for the lead. Rudy had slammed the Spook in the North turn and was able to get by him on the straight as the thin number 30 driver lost valuable seconds correcting for Rudy's blow. Pat on the inside, was running abreast of Rudy on the next lap, the Spook planting the red one on the Hudson's tail. In the next turn, he bumped Pat rather hard, again, at the adhesion point. Pat, correcting for the bump, turned squarely in front of Rudy. This left an open hole on the inside that the Spook so readily took advantage of the little 30 car dancing gingerly into the lead.

At several points during the remainder of the contest it looked as though one of my Hudsons or Rudy and his teammates, might ace the red 30 out on one of the straights. This never came about. That determined ghostlike figure and his screaming red machine were as one. Keeping the lead the remainder of the conflict. The Plymouths little engine was always drowned out by our bigger bore Hudson's and the Olds V-8's beside operating at top revs. If you have ever heard an engine wound tight, so high that it is nearly silent, you can easily fathom how the Spook's Plymouth sounded. Besides being smothered by the big cars, number 30 was always running at those super silent revolutions. It didn't mean anything really, but just lent a bit more eeriness to that strange, icy figure known only as the Spook.

The Olds factory, depending on Rudy to take first that Sunday in order to boost their point lead over the Hudson teams, were very disappointed. I won't forget the surprised hurt look that Rudy's manager gave him as he climbed from the cockpit of the disheveled Rocket. Rudy's thoughts, however, were far from any team manager's feelings, as Miss Mary planted a long kiss on the quivering lips of the Spook...

As many other managers, I had approached the Spook to drive on my team. One day he came in, wanting to look the Hudson's over. We ventured out into the shop and over to Jerry's car parked near the grease pit. He climbed through the window, as the doors on competition cars are bolted shut for safety reasons, and began a mock race making up and down shifts with the gear selector.

I said nothing for a while, but watched the far-away look on his face as he reefed on the wheel to avoid an imaginary opponent.

"You were sure pushing that yellow Olds in that last turn, Spook," I finally said. He, in his courteous way, more or less dismissed me then, continuing his make-believe contest. He signed on with us for the next race up in Rudy's home stomping grounds at Polson.

He worked side by side with Elmer and George to prepare another Hudson in time for Polson. Due to his insistence, the car he was to drive was numbered 30. We had planned to number the car 24, as we already had the two preceding numbers, but we hesitated to cross him, least we lose him to another organization. Number 30 set the pace that following Sunday, pinning the Olds team down in their own living room. Our other cars finished well too, and Tom and I were elated at the fine start we had made that season. Nor was that the end of our winning streak as we were blessed with one at Morgantown and no less than two over at the Fairview Track, each time the Spook showing the way.

He spearheaded the Hudson's that whole season. I guess I was about the happiest guy on the circuit at the close of that racing year, when our annual 500-miler, marking the finish of the year's action, was won also by the Spook.

Bob French of headquarters called, informing me that he had been advised by the Hudson factory of a new model already in production in Detroit! The new model dubbed the Hudson Hornet was to deliver a true 145 horsepower at 4000 RPM and substantial torque increase too featuring dual carburetion, larger bore and ignition modification along with a faster camshaft, the mill was an answer to all our prayers.

The growing threat of the Olds Rocket and its breath taking

acceleration were probably a prime factor in the factory's decision to introduce the Hornet. The Hornet was favored by technical sources to be stock car king of the circuits approaching 51 Conflict.

Some alarming news, centered around the Chrysler Corporation reached us the following day. The big Chrysler apparently anxious to reap some of the Laurels already won by its smaller brother, the Plymouth was announcing their 51 models with an entirely different engine. A large bore V type hemi head, said to produce over two hundred horsepower, an unheard figure at that time. Displacing 331 cubic inches and with tremendous torque. That monstrosity may well deal us all considerable headaches. Olds too was not standing idle and proclaimed more power for the rocket series. Detroit was flexing its muscles.

Bob phoned again a week later with some surprising information. Always a jump ahead of everyone on future developments, he was a highly reliable source in our ever changing circles.

The commencing of the 51 season was to be a road race over the sports car course near Morgantown.

"A road race for stockers Bob, You're joking" "So help me Bill, that's gospel straight from the highest brass."

Events were really shaping up and I felt, and always had, that a road race was a far more rugged test of man and machine. What about the drivers, men accustomed to negotiating continuous left hand turns may find it difficult to adapt themselves to the twisting esses, snap bendsand and other familiar tricks of the hay baled lined sports car course.

It was evident too, that the stockers would undergo a far greater stress. Brakes, I thought, would be the principal failure, but the other components would doubtless suffer also.

I looked with confidence to the willing and able hands of Elmer and George for the long grind of car preparation.

The first day that the weather cleared in early spring we assembled the crew together on the track.

It had been a long drawn out winter. Since the news of the road react first reached us. Elmer had just turned loose the hornets and we all watched in expectation as the Spook and Buck mounted up.

They cut a full two seconds off of our previous lap times, and on the spooks third time over the track with the number 30 hornet, he broke his own track record set at the 500 miler the year before.

The Hornets would really charge out of the corners and had an impressive top speed.

Their handling characteristics were without fault.

Sitell's Exhaust Note was located two blocks from the speed way. We all stopped there, on numerous occasions, for a brew, or a shot of scotch from his elaborate cocktail lounge. On this particular evening, the Note was half full of paying customers, all feeling nicely aglow. Rudy Lock and Miss Mary were seated in a booth with another couple, perhaps fifty feet from the bar, where Jerry, Buck and I were seated, discussing strategy for the coming friction on the Morgantown road course. Laughter and the clatter of near empty glasses assailed my ears from the direction of Rudy's small group, the latter's own booming voice drowning out those of the others. We had been talking and drinking for nearly an hour and they had arrived before us, drinking far more potent stuff.

I surmised that they were pretty well "airborne." That is, except Miss Mary, who seldom drank.

Over against the far wall, other members of the Olds team had gathered, speaking in hushed, secretive tones.

As the evening wore on, a solitary drinker set himself down, a few stools from us, his head bowed in thought.

Although the Spook was known to tip one up on a hot day, he didn't party like some of the drivers did. His chalky countenance matched that of the clean, white coveralls he was wearing as he entered the semi-darkened atmosphere of the smoke-filled cocktail lounge. There was definitely an electric tenseness about him that was felt throughout the entire room.

As he slid onto a stool at the bar, the solitary drinker, upon glancing at him, jerked swiftly away, as if receiving a physical blow from some unseen source. Miss Mary, much to Rudy's annoyance, cast frequent, questing gazes at the pale, silent figure. I motioned him to join us and he gave that polite nod… remaining where he was.

The Spook was beyond our comprehension. At times, he seemed to be one of us, a racer, loving the high reviving Husdons, the stench of burning rubber, the exhilaration of seeing all the cars lined up in the pit area awaiting the drivers. Even the crack of bare knuckles against steel as a wrench grip slipped. Then there were the times like that evening in the Note, when he seemed as distant as the first place finish of an independent entry, during those hectic days of team domination. It had been too early in my racing experience for me to realize that there was a man whose very existence depended on speed. His whole life his very all, was the circuit. To be out of the cascading machines for one hour, one moment, meant a lonely void that nothing or no one could fill. But, as the shining eyes of Miss Mary turned on him once more, I wondered if the possibility were there for a person, a wonderful person like Mary, to crash that solid, forlorn wall that was him, the Spook. I had witnessed those glowing green eyes in silent conversation with the terrible, piercing eyes of him, and I had seen those bottomless pits soften and show life. A life that didn't depend on the split second timing and hundred mile an hour wail of a thrashing Hudson, sizzling down the straightaway. Rather, they had shown a light for that charming girl in the royalty section. There could be no doubt in my mind as to the destiny of those two. How little I understood what fate had in store for the future, leaving a far emptier void for both of them.

The treacherous Rudy ordered another round, rose, apparently heading for the men's room, his ever present smirk magnifying with each step he took toward the seated Spook. I think Rudy realized his mistake, judging by the shocked expression he had on his drink-reddened face, as the Spook turned around after being prodded in the spine by Rudy's elbow. Everyone in the house saw the play, some for it, some neither way. Rudy had had something on his twisted mind ever since that very first race, when the Spook had taken away his prestige within one or two laps.

With a sufficient whiskey courage boost Rudy braced that slim quiet figure. In his loud, crude way he rasped "Excuses me, creep" gave a sneer on top of his smirk and started away. No one saw the tight, white fist shoot into Rudy's belly. One moment the Spook was on the stool, the next he was standing, cutting Rudy to ribbons with precise slashing blows. Rudy doubled over from the shock of the onslaught concentrated against his mid-section and received a bashing knee in the face and a double-handed rabbit punch, simultaneously. The bulk of his big body went limp and was like soft putty, his arms flailing as he crashed to the floor accompanied by two more cutting blows to his already bruised and bleeding face! How could that have happened within the space of so few seconds.. It was incredible! The relatively slender Spook completely destroying a beefy hulk of a man like Rudy. The whole house were on their feet, staring in disbelief at the tornado-like event unfolded before them. Had not Rudy been noted as a bar room tough and on countless occasions whipped two and even three men his own size all at once? How then could he have fallen so swiftly never so much as casting a single blow?

As if on a given signal, the Olds team swarmed in at him six strong! Jerry, Buck, and I dis-liking the odds, jockeyed for combat. Our stumbling efforts were not needed however, for in a flash he snatched a handful of shuffleboard cues and began bombarding his assailants with deadly accuracy. A red cue took a driver-mechanic squarely betwixt the eyes dropping the man like a pole axed critter at the stock yards. A blue cue smashed another attacker and he went down. I had visions of cracked skulls all over the place.

The women, panicked, added to the din of the scrap with their senseless screaming. Only one of the original six got through to him, whereas he received the same slashing and cutting attack administered to Rudy. The man went down twisting on the floor, but the Spook in an uncontrollable fury still lashed him, dragging the man to his feet, hammering down again! As I got my wits about me, I rushed in to stop him before he should kill or maim the man. With superhuman strength, he threw me off like a toy... and then his deadly, black gaze met that of Miss Mary. Again their glances locked for what seemed an eternity, the time limit accentuated because of the tomblike stillness of the room.

You could actually see that terrible fire in him subside and then quench itself altogether. She stared long seconds at the vacant opening, long seconds after he passed through as if some magnetic force compelled her to do so. The glowing green eyes were shining in all their brilliance and not once did she look toward the crumpled Rudy who lay in painful sleep.

Someone called an ambulance and we began gathering up the bruised, torn flesh left in the furious wake of him, the Spook!

Standing rather tall, there in the living room, while Mart adjusted her fluttering red evening dress, I marveled at her beauty. My wife, Marty, was a living, breathing doll in her own way, but looked almost plain, despite her makeup, as she fussed and feathered around the classic Mary. Mary's light face, accentuated by her raven black hair, and those lovely, green eyes that shone so brightly that afternoon, their intensity suggesting a far deeper beauty, that of inner soul and spirit. Again, I found myself comparing her steady, untroubled gaze, to that of him, the Spook, whose won gaze was so intense, but in that terrifying, deadly way.

"Still that fire, Mary. Use whatever means that you can muster but still it. For such an unearthly force cannot stay inside him much longer and unless it is destroyed, it will destroy." I was surprised to hear Mary answer, "I know, Bill." The bright green eyes wavered and for the whisper of a second, a clouded hidden fear showed.

"Well, please let me in on it." Marty said, tilting her head at a funny little angle, as she always did when she was amiss of what was being shuffled to and fro, in a serious conversation.

"You and Bill have been such grand friends. You should be the first to know." " Marty, I love him, I love him so much." The girls embraced Marty half sobbing in happiness.

"Little Mary, I knew that you would have a love affair before this year was out. I'm so glad for you." Marty turned on all her graciousness, her face tear-streaked with tears of understanding. All the grandeur was there in that small, sparkling countenance that had drawn me to her and turned me from a selfish, self-centered businessman to a puppet at her instant command. If she asked for the Empire State Building, I would do my damndest to get it for her. Only that was just it. Mart never asked for anything and was content to let me do all the deciding, but would always suggest, or try and help me in any way that I needed her and needed her I did so very much. I would bring her home some trivial gift at times, the look she gave me as I handed her the small token holding me spellbound for two weeks. We really had something, Mart and I. Something that we could never lose. I swallowed a sore lump in my throat as I was asked a question.

"Sure, sure, Mary, I'm happy for you too, you know only too well how I am."

"Bill, that makes it unanimous, so now you must help me land my man."

"Me Mary?" I asked.

"You Bill. Tell me a little about him, for he speaks so seldom of himself, I know nothing. Of course, we've only been out a few times. He seems so keyed up Bill. What is it with Spook....how can I help him? Ever since that first race, when he looked at me, I've known. He is everything that I want Bill."

"Just be you Mary. That will give him all the help he needs."

"Sometimes, I can't understand him. He's so far away at times that I can't seem to break the wall down between us. It's almost like...well, he must have a deep devotion for another woman, and he isn't sure if it's me he wants....or her."

Oh no, I thought to myself. She doesn't fathom the Spook's

other love at all. I had misinterpreted the shining glow in her eyes that first day, when they spoke in silent conversation. True, her love for him was real, but I had failed to note that she didn't understand the terrible turmoil in his eyes and his passion for the chance and risk of the circuit. How could I possibly explain it to her?

Marty knew, she always knew about everything like that.

I shook my head at her, making movements with my lips in the form of I love you. She forced a nervous smile and lent the finishing touches to Mary's trousseau.

"Listen Mary, give him a lot of time, and when you're with him be light hearted as you can. He'll come around. I'm sure of it." I somehow wondered if time was not a limited factor, but shook my head again. You've got a great imagination Nordic, you should be a writer, I criticized myself.

The Spook, with Mary, looked like any of the others in the room. The deep pits that were his eyes had a contented glow in them that was present when he was near Mary. Marty saw it too, nodding in approval. There was that taut, unsure feeling about her where he, the Spook was concerned, but I could understand, for I too had my chill feelings when he was involved, although I never told Marty that.

Rudy was there, red faced as ever, with Flora Young from over near Tyson, and was strangely sober! If I hadn't been there and saw it myself, I would never had believed it. Possibly, he had begun to grow up.

The look on his face, when Mary and the Spook entered the Star Room, was one of defeat, bitterness and I think resolution. What form of resolution I wasn't sure. But knowing Rudy, there would have to be something conniving involved.

Rudy whispered something to Flora, rose, and started toward his arch enemy and rival, both on and away from the speedways.

All eyes turned on the hulk that was Rudy Lock, as he trod nearly the full length of the slippery dance floor and his slender objective. Marty stiffened, glanced with wide eyes at me, then to Mary and him, the Spook.

Although showing no apparent awareness of Rudy's approach, the Spook was observing him carefully, and by the time he had arrived had swung Mary in such a way that he might face Rudy squarely. Rudy, familiar with such tactical advantages himself, grinned crookedly through big, white teeth that were too even and straight to be real. He held up an ape like hand in gesture of truce I leaned forward, hoping to pick up a piece of the conversation.

"Deck him, Spook! Deck him and stomp on him!"

"What did you say Bill?" Oh, nothing Mart. I was just wondering what they were saying, that's all"

"NUTS." Rudy smiled at Miss Mary, nodded politely to the Spook and asked for the next dance. It didn't seem possible that Rudy could have anything but foul play on his warped mind, but made no underhanded moves, as the Spook surrendered Mary to his outstretched hand.

I wondered how Rudy would finally act to Mary's being chaperoned by the Spook.

Surely, he would know well enough…to keep a safe distance from the icy figure, but then again, Rudy was the bullheadest of men. Although it was wrong of me to hope for a fight, I would have so much liked to have seen the calculative movements and methodical blows administered to Rudy again. Not that I felt any worse toward him that previously, but rather, to see the symphonic actions of the Spook in physical combat was an education that one does not encounter often. Marty would club me if I so much as mentioned such an atrocity, so I doused the little light in my noggin.

The music stopped, the various couples filing to their respective tables, several remaining standing for the next number. I sat there next to Mart, soaking in the refrains of the dashing arrangement of "You go to my Head" with some of the lyrics that I liked; such as "You intoxicate my soul with your eyes".

Had the Spook known that Rudy was not going to make a scene, as was his usual method? If so, how? What a vast knowledge of human psychology that pale man possessed. Nothing, it seemed, was too much for him to comprehend. That instance was just one of the many, where he clearly demonstrated his remarkable perception of human reasoning. Why, if he was so strong in that knowledge, did he let himself be engulfed with that terrible driving force...

He stood there alone for a moment, watching Miss Mary be swept away by Rudy, then turned, facing us. I looked at Marty, she nodded in assent and I motioned him over. He came, and unfamiliar pleasantness about him, bowed gallantly to Marty, shook my hand and was seated.

He was full of chatter for the small, ordinarily unobserved things. Things that such as him never would give a thought to. A new side of this extraordinary person was unveiled, a happy, peaceful side, and Marty never once removed her eyes from his interesting face. I was appalled by the striking difference from the Spook that I knew on the circuit, and this...this...other self that was showing itself. How long would this new side remain...and if the new personality should stay with him, what of the circuit?

This other self might well be unable to maintain top position in the constant hassle with the factory teams.

What kind of creep was I turning into...thinking of the Spook in terms of a machine? Hell, I was the one who was being carried away. For an instance, I looked at him only as a business asset, when in reality he was the greatest man I had ever met.

"You aren't listening, Bill," Marty said, as I found her and the Spook staring at me in open amusement.

"I think my friend Bill is contemplating our next race. No need to worry, Bill. Nothing has changed." The silvery depth of his eyes told me that he knew my thoughts.

After flustering around, I finally got out a few weak words. "I'm glad , Spook"

"What in heaven's name are you two talking about? Marty asked. She looked at me, then the Spook. I looked at her and then the Spook. He gave that polite nod, stood up and sauntered over to Mary. I scratched my jaw that didn't really itch and ordered another drink. Rudy's good will held through the evening and I nursed the idea as to what might be accomplished with Rudy and the Spook on the same team. That is if Rudy's sudden change of heart was genuine.

Unfortunately, as I had suspected, Rudy's change of heart was false. The 250 lap main event over at Polson the following Sunday bore witness to that. The Chryslers had been giving both of them trouble on the straights and constant changes in positions had been taking place. The Spook, who had been running third be-hind Buck and Rudy crowded hard in the North turn, putting the Hornet on the rail and holding it there at eighty miles per hour. Buck gave ground, but Rudy had to be tapped rather sharply before he swung his potent Rocket to the side. At midway of the race the Spook was leading.

The next lap saw two of the factory Fords blow up because of the terrific times that were being turned in. That left the main show with the Hornets and Rockets, an occasional Plymouth sneaking into contention. The Chryslers ran well in the beginning of the race, but had been side lined with an assortment of ailments, common with the introduction of a new engine. When the technical bugs were worked out of those machines, we would all be in trouble. There fine showing on the Morgantown road course proved that much.

Rudy was right on the Spooks tail and up until then it appeared we were to have a good clean contest all the way through. He made a spectacular bid for the lead and was successful cutting the number 30 Hornet out in the North turn slipping in behind the one remaining Chrysler.

All that was fine. Rudy for once showing signs of magnificent sportsman ship. As he passed cars he waved, or if he was passed, he made the same gesture. Then it happened!

The Spook had pulled into the pits for fuel and right side tires relinquishing his lead to Rudy, Buck, and a Ford driver. The efficient pit crew, sent to us by the factory, had the number 30 car ready to go in seconds. As he accelerated back on the track, Rudy, who had signaled for a pit stop on the previous lap and had actually begun to slow and turn into his spot, saw the Spook pulling out and decided to wait. He cracked the Rocket into first gear and with engine screaming in over revs, slammed the Hornet a glancing blow! The Spooks tie rod had been knocked off in the fracas and the Hornet careened into the Ford pits, knocking over several cans of fuel that suddenly ignited, sending mechanics scampering in every direction for cover.

Number 30 had caught fire and before the Spook could get clear, his arms were burned and he was overcome by smoke.

Rudy's gloating over the incident nearly cost him his license. At that, he was fined a large sum and suspended for three events. The Association was sore, and with good reason at such deliberate foulness. Of course Rudy said it had been an accident that "the creep" had pulled out in front of him.

The Olds factory saved his hide from total expulsion, but the big ignoramus appeared not in the least grateful.

Upon visiting the Spook at Mercy Hospital, I found Mary by his side, crying softly. I felt like an intruder, but he beckoned me over to him. As he looked up at me, his face matching the shade of the clean starched pillow, the softness of his features the night of the Association dance were gone, and once more the terrible eyes were present. He motioned toward Miss Mary, then the door, and I walked over taking her arm and leading her from the antiseptic smell of the small room.

Poor Mary. She was so broken up at the thought of losing him. That near miss had really shaken her. I decided that it was time to tell her of the Spook and what the circuit was to him. I got it all out to the smallest detail and was rather surprised at the easiness and the rolling note to my voice.

When I finished, there was a long silence as Mary seemed to be fighting for the right words. She then asked "Would he leave the circuit for me Bill?" I was always asked those dilly type questions that were so difficult to answer. "Have you asked him Mary?" "No, I'm afraid to now Bill. What if he should say that he couldn't?"

As much as the circuit was to him, I was sure that he would leave it for her. After seeing that the green eyes could calm him, I was positive of it. My insight to that fascinating man was small though and he could and did surprise me every day with some new part of him. Was it my place to give Mary an answer then? Why the hell is it that everything that you do involves human emotions? Couldn't everybody just be a good guy and we all would get along?

"I think he would Mary, but I'm not sure."

She looked pained by my blunt reply and said, "Oh Bill, I can't lose him." She hung her head and began to cry again.

That same chill wind was with us, as I took Mary's arm and we left the hospital.

When he was released from the hospital a short time later, I was surprised to find that the terrible eyes were not with him. Mary meant that much to him then, enough to stave that smoldering fire inside him, enough to give him a contented look even after Rudy's deliberate attempt to destroy him. Yes, I expected to see a wrathful youth emerge from that white bed at Mercy Hospital, instead finding much to my happiness a perfectly calm, or apparently so, Spook. Could it have been that he secretly planned Rudy's destruction in his heart, putting all those concerned at ease with his nonchalance? This I pondered with serious thought.

I think Mary was ready to ask him to quit the circuit, but I'm not sure. A powder puff derby was scheduled for our track the following month, Mary Jacobs name as an entry. That figured. She would never ask him to quit without first going over to his side of the picture. I guess she just wanted to prove to him that she could do as well as the other gals, but that it was no life to lead after a marriage. At any rate, he was instructing her in the art of race driving the old red Plymouth that we first saw him in, the number 30 fading on its scuffed and scarred side.

Day after day, the little engine sang around the deserted speedway and it sounded almost like the little red car had a heart somewhere inside its torn, metal fatigued body. As the days progressed, Mary rapidly got the feel of the asphalt circle, making laps comparable to the Spooks own times. Of course, on an empty track it was far different than the heated skirmishing of all out racing.

After about three of these instructions he took the number 30 Hornet over and ran with her. I went over to watch, just to see how Mary was doing. It was an odd feeling to see two number 30 cars on the track, almost like tempting fate, I thought. Oh, what the hell was wrong with me? It was just her and the Spook were so much together and I didn't want anything to happen. That's all.

They drove in an abreast formation for a couple of laps, then he took the leading position, setting a swift pace for her to follow. She broke the Plymouth loose a time or two correcting, feathering the throttle nicely.

They sped down the straight and he allowed her to come abreast once more. They accelerated in unison and accomplished the maneuver in the following turn, the Spook sliding the Hornet within inches of the slab sided Plymouth.

Mary grim determination on her face, budged not an inch, instead, chopping the Spook off as they spun through the corner. As a finale to her education, he followed her around the track, bumping her roughly in the turns. That bumping action; that was her weakest point. She seemed to panic, neglecting to correct as quickly as she should.

He followed her around again and again, slamming her harder in the turns with each lap, until it appeared that she was over the fear of that jarring, neck snapping action.

The Association had started an amateur division for all the up and coming new drivers. These amateur contests usually consisted of two fifty lap events. The Powder Puff Derby was scheduled, in addition to the regular race for Saturday afternoon and all the gals with pit crews were gathering since daybreak at the speedway. The Spook was acting the part of safety man, driving the 00 car. A red Ram Dodge. Whenever one of the contestants was in trouble, engine failure, or the like, well, he would push them off the track.

Although the gals were limited to small displacement engines they put on a spectacular show. There were fifteen entries in all, Plymouths, Fords, Chevs and a scattering of other makes.

Rudy's current girl friend, Betty Hunter, was there and copped second spot in the time trials, Mary making first. Betty was a far more aggressive driver than Mary, that is, in the tight places. If there was a risk of someone going into the wall in a crowded turn, Mary would slack off, giving the other driver a break. Betty, on the other hand, schooled in the methods of the self considerate Rudy Lock, would never give an inch. She was there to win, no holds barred!

The Spook drover the 00 car to the head of the pack, the contestants starting their engines…it was time.

Betty, driving her Chevy, was pushing Mary at every opportunity, on the tenth lap of the fifty lapper, stealing the lead from her in the South turn.

The other gals couldn't match the scorching pace and were battling amongst themselves for third place.

Rudy was jumping up and down on the sidelines, frantically waving at Betty to pour on the coal. She increased her lead on Mary by nearly half a lap and it looked as though she may well be the victor. Mary held her own, little by little filling the gap that separated them. By lap forty she was in contention and began to bump Betty in the turns. Rudy had taught the honey blond girl well, for with each bump administered her by Mary, she corrected splendidly with the steering!

The two cars were geared pretty nearly the same, accelerating down the straight abreast. Mary gave up the bumping routine and shot around Betty on the outside of the next turn, swerving in front of her and taking over the lead at the beginning of the forty-fifth lap. Betty held the Chevy glued to the Plymouth's bumper, slamming it a hefty one in the north turn. Mary came close to spinning out, but caught the car in the nick of time. I watched her intently through my glasses and it seemed as though the green eyes had a fleck of those terrible eyes of the Spook in them. Mary was mad now! She fishtailed the Plymouth on the straight, bashing the Chevy a solid blow, as the latter tried to force her off the track. Betty slowed then, and with one lap remaining, was four or five lengths behind the angry Plymouth and a spooky Miss Mary.

A spin out by one of the other girls caused Mary to slow, Betty once again challenging as the two cars broke out of the south turn together.

Having nearly halted for the disabled car, it was a case of a drag race to see who was to take the lead once more and win the race.

With a faster ratio first gear and a rolling start, Mary surged ahead of the Chevy, only to be caught as the two were winding out in second gear.

Betty wound the Chevy up to an ear piercing fifty in second and moved the shift lever to third...She missed! There was a rasping, grating scratch. She cracked it back to second again, stomping on the throttle!

Mary wound out to a screaming fifty-five in second, and on shifting to third, the race was hers.

About a minute later, she pulled the Plymouth into the pits after making the winner's circle. The Spook was laughing like a big kid. Appearing well prepared and confident of victory, the Olds team made their appearance at the road course around eleven thirty with the well proven Yellow Rockets. We were pinning our hopes on the swift, but as yet unproven Hornets. Factory observers had noticed that the Super Rocket Olds answer to the Hudson Hornet, had shown a defiant case of fuel starvation in short, flat corners. Unless this disadvantage was corrected, our sleek Hornets, with their improved performance, may well deal the Olds stable a bitter defeat. The greatest threat, we felt, was from the Chrysler Organization.

Tom and I had watched two of Jud Morgan's, of the Valley Chrysler-Plymouth agency; chase one another over the twisting course. With goliath acceleration, they would easily be first out of the corners. But what of going into the curves in the first place... This, we felt, was where the Hornets had them all.

Our marked performance gains would not excel those of the Chrysler, but would be sufficient to shadow the big brutes at a closing distance on the straights, dashing around them in the turns.

With eighteen cars competing on the two mile course, four

were our Hornets, three olds, three Plymouths, four Fords, two each Dodge and Mercury. It was interesting to note the complete domination by factory backed teams. There were only a few independent entries on the scene.

Time trials found Rudy Lock, still bearing scars from his fight with the Spook, found, on pole position. The Spook and Jerry made the second and third spots, while a Chrysler and another Rocket filled fourth and fifth. Buck and Pat, due to spin outs, fell far to the rear of the field.

The rising and falling pulse beats of the big bore mills set ones blood to tingling, exhaust smoke, that stank of too rich fuel mixtures, filling the air, stinging the nostrils. Pit crewman and spectators alike jumped and cheered with released tensions and expectations, as the green flag was dropped.

Black smudges left oversized tires with a complaining squeal attaching themselves to the concrete of the long home stretch, as the racers catapulted forward!

The Spook stayed beside Rudy's Olds, proved to all the marked acceleration gains of the Hornets over 50 models.

The first five cars remained closely bunched, arriving at turn number one in a pack! The Spook and Rudy held full throttle until the last second, sliding dangerously close clear through the turn. Those two rivals continued their risky abreast formation, steadily increasing their lead over the rest of the field. Shifting down for a series of esses, Rudy missed a cog or two, the gears making considerable grinding noise. The Olds driver succeeded on his second try, but had to brake sharply.

The Spook wasn't out to watch the bold Rudy practicing shifting, promptly edging him out and taking over the lead. He goosed the Hornet in the right hand bend of the esses, the whipping motion nearly breaking the more powerful machine loose. In the same fashion, Jerry spun his Hornet out, thus allowing the big Chrysler and Rudy's teammate to get in front of him. He recovered the Hornet quickly and set out to harry the two aggressive opponents.

On the backstretch, Rudy slowly pulled up on the Spook, who was lashing the Hornet mercilessly. It was a neck and neck run, the Rocket slowing passing and taking over the lead before the next series of esses were reached.

Seeing that the Rocket was going to pass him anyway, the Spook relinquished his lead, cutting sharply behind the swift Olds. He rode the big Olds driver hard, hoping to panic him by his fractional nearness. Rudy held on, boring onto the home stretch in a well controlled power slide.

The fantastic Spook slipped by Rudy once again on the inside, his Hornet in an actual four wheel drift! They were again abreast coming down the home straight, in excess of one hundred miles per hour!

Even the sports car drivers, skeptical of the stocker's ability to put on any kind of a show on a road course, had their mouths agape in wonder and astonishment.

A new kind of stock car competition was being born and I was proud to be a part of it.

At midpoint of the heated contest, only eight cars were still active, five of which were in contention of one another. The tight, hot course was truly taking its toll in failing clutches, brakes, burned out rear ends, blown engines and seized gear boxes.

The Spook slid into the pits for fuel and a change of rubber, Rudy and the big Chrysler whistling by. In only a matter of seconds the Hornet roared and was ready to go. The shattering pace must have been sapping him, for as the 30 car swept by me, face helmet and snow white uniform were blended into one as the still vapor like form guided the surging Hudson ahead with swift, flowing shifts.

Mary and Marty were keeping a close tab on the swift racers, in particular, the number 30, which had began to leave a faint trail of smoke behind. The haze increased with each terrific lap and the Hornet seemed to falter in some of the turns, the Chrysler and Rudy gaining steadily. With one remaining lap, that deadly banner developed into nothing less than a cloud of black smoke. The engine was going to shatter!

If only the car will last, I prayed. I followed the relentless lecherous stream in my glasses as number 30 was pushed for all that was in it!

Rudy and the big number 4 Chrysler, sensing the plight of the dying Hornet, rapidly closed the gap separating them. Jerry had out maneuvered the number five Chrysler in the S bends and was scrapping it out with Rudy's teammate for forth position.

If only we could pull this off, I found myself chanting! They roared down the home stretch in an oily, dark cloud, a staggering Hornet, a determined Rudy, and the big, predatory Chrysler. It was to be close... Oh, so close... Smoke, dust...fumes...He had done it...He had done it!!

Hail the Spook!

Jerry shot in only a fraction of a second ahead of the other Olds, netting us a hard earned first and forth for the day.

Fire extinguishers spat at the base of the flames under the dejected Hornet...number 30!

How he had managed to breathe inside that gloomy, broiling tomb I'll never know. But, then maybe he didn't need air like an average person does, for he was certainly far from average in every respect. I grinned at my cleverness, but the private jest was soon forgotten as I found myself observed by the terrible eyes of him, the Spook!

Gulping a deep breath of my own, I rushed forth to congratulate him…

The racing world had acknowledged the Spook as the greatest driver in the history of late model competition. We were flooded with mail from well wishers and enthusiasts down at Nordic and Clark Motors, requesting his autograph and snap shot. The sallow cheeks had grown even more gaunt and he seldom ever slept, then only half hour catnaps.

I was proud along with everyone on our team, of his achievements and the humble attitude he took when being praised, but he would have to slow from the murdering pace which was driving him, lest he become seriously ill. We wanted him to lay off for a couple of races but not so. He won the scorching 300 miler at Fairview, the following weekend, laboring all through the night with Elmer and George in order to have the 30 car properly prepared.

He was part of that Hornet in all its actions, passing competition anywhere, sometimes at seemingly impossible places. How long could he last in the hands of that "recklessness" that pursued him unceasingly…? I found myself wishing that Mary would take him into tow, quenching that unseen, driving force that drove him before it misled him and destroyed him.

Such were my disturbing thoughts when the Hornet ruled the circuit and want or need of any material thing was unthought-of. Yes, we were rolling in good fortune in those early days, parties and get together often.

A pair of Kiekhaefer cars — Chrysler 300 and Dodge 500 — sweep around a turn in typical formation on their way to cleaning up a one-two finish. This familiar scene will not be repeated at stock car tracks.

IN DAYS GONE BY: At the Portland Speedway Half-Mile Track in June, 1962 . . . No. 27, Bob Gregg spins out and is passed by Johnny Frederick, who goes on to win the race in No. 30 . . . (inset) Johnny Frederick, in his car-racing heyday.

SPIRIT

YOU KNOW ABOUT NASCAR AND THE BIG
RACING ORGANIZATIONS...

YOU KNOW ABOUT THE FANTASTIC
200MPH DRIVERS...

NOW IT IS TIME...

NOW IT IS TIME THAT YOU KNOW HOW IT
ALL BEGAN...

NOW IT IS TIME FOR...

THE SPIRIT

by

Johnny Frederick

MEET THE ELECTRIFYING CHARACTER
KNOWN ONLY AS *SPOOK* PERHAPS THE
GREATEST DRIVER IN THE WORLD...

FROM THE SINGING SIXES...TO THE
DETROIT SUPERCARS...HE WAS MASTER
OF THEM ALL...

WATCH FOR...
"ABLE DOG"
(THE WAR THAT NEVER ENDED)
COMING IN---
2010/12
FROM THE AUTHOR OF THE
"SPIRIT"

AD SKYRAIDER invites attention wherever it appears.

The long anticipation that we all had for the Hudson V8 was doomed. The factory didn't say when there would be a new engine, go to hell or anything. We were all hoping for an engine like the Chrysler hemi.

They did produce the new engine, but it was too late and we had lost out title and were never again to be the celebrity of the circuit.

I think I can truthfully state that we did maintain our crown in the 51 season.

"All right, by damn, I had said, we will fight them to the death. We did fight them too, and we lost, but our competitors always knew that we were there and, they had to give it their all in order to beat us!!!

Following that born leader, the Spook, the boys worked out some track tactics that proved successful many times.

The writing was there through and out beloved Hornets began to fail. Even him, even the Spook, could no longer fight off the big, snarling V's...We were in trouble...

When the Hornets had lost their place at the summit of the winning list in late 1953 there had been several heated discussions between my partner, Tom Clark, the board of directors, and myself, of dissolving the team. From a business standpoint, it was the move to make, especially since factory aid had been growing weaker, but I had not the heart for it. I know the Spook and the other boys had various offers from the victorious teams of Olds, Dodge and Chrysler, but I also knew of their unquestionable loyalty. We had no right to hold them though, for they had always done far more than was expected of them. But with them gone we had no chance at all for survival.

With continuing losses on the circuit, a heavy drop in sales took place. It was getting rather tight around the collar and in a meeting with the board in October of 1953, it was decided to terminate the actions of the team. I sure hated to see such a precision organization disbanded, but it had to be done. I could hardly feature myself content to go about the routine of an ordinary salesman again and told Tom so.

Tom was very understanding, offering to buy my stock in our dealership. We had been associated for years and I hated to dissolve our relationship without further thought on the matter. So, with a heavy heart I scheduled a meeting with the drivers for the following day at Sitell's Exhaust Note.

I arrived a little earlier than I had designated for the boys to meet me, contemplating to reinforce myself with a stiff belt or two of that imported Scotch that Nick was always boasting about.

I pulled up behind Nick's black Dodge convertible, revved the Hudson up a time or two and switched it off.

Nick was seated at the bar sampling some of his own wares, when I plodded in.

"Come on over and plant yourself, Bill" he said. "Why the hell are you looking so glum? Those Hornets aren't doing that bad."

"It's worse than you think Nick. We've dissolved the team."

"No, Bill!" He exclaimed, an astonished look on his thick-jowled face. Nick Sitell had purchased a Hudson from us every year since he had built the Exhaust Note, until '54, when he had succumbed to the V trend.

"Hell Bill, the Hornets aren't beaten yet, they'll make a comeback."

I looked squarely at him, replying, "You weren't sure enough to buy another one, were you Nick?" His mouth was agape as the accuracy of my statement struck home.

"No offense, Nick" I had gone on. "It's just that the wins on the circuit are what is selling cars nowadays. People have become very conscious of what their car is doing on the race track, not that there is any similarity to a "set up" stocker and what the average joker wheels away from the stop light in. Do you follow me Nick?"

Yeah, I know how it is from hearing the drivers talking." He poured a generous portion of dark liquid in my near empty glass.

The average man, too, has no idea that competition cars are especially prepared for the grueling pounding of the track. They think, when they see a Hudson or a Dodge whizzing around a circle track, or over a road course, that it is just like theirs…If the car wins, they can tell all their friends with inferior makes, that they drive a car "*just like the one that won the race Sunday.*"

Then they'll climb into their car, stomp it to the floor and blast off through town, usually ending up in some tavern or at the local pokey, or both.

Outside tires screeched and the sound of well timed down shifts drifted through the open window. The team had arrived and I steeled myself for the unpleasant job ahead.

They swallowed the news with no apparent shock, but I could feel the disappointment heavy in the clouded atmosphere of a room that had begun to fill with the early evening trade. The Spook signaled for a round and we raised our glasses in salute to the screaming Hornets that had carried us all so far. Despite Nick's high priced scotch, the bitter taste of defeat was in all our mouths. I turned to the Spook to ask him of his plans and found him gone.

An engine was winding high out front, our glances all piercing the front window and deepening twilight at once. The red

Plymouth shouted at the gloom in the air, the number 30 on its bright side seeming to magnify with each revolution of the tiny power plant.

A white arm extending from its black interior, waved in a gesture of encouragement, as the Plymouth accelerated into the growing darkness.

What an odd way to leave, we all thought. Then, as an afterthought, I guess it wasn't so strange, not for him, not for the Spook.

With the dispersal of the team, I could not adapt myself to the routine of selling Hudsons and accepted Tom's offer to buy me out. We parted on the best of terms and I'll respect him for himself and his solid judgment.

Morgantown lies sixty miles Southeast of Norfolk and it was there Marty and I moved. Mart was sorry to leave all her many friends in Norfolk, but never complained. What a wonderful girl. She knew that the circuit had taken little of myself away from her, but nary a murmur.

I guess that I had become somewhat like the Spook, with the exception that I didn't drive. One doesn't have to actually compete there on the track in one of the highly tuned cars, for the bewitching spell of that swiftest of all sports, to burrow into your very self and engulf you with its startling, unpredictable and often times, disastrous moods. For every lap a car finishes, you can be sure that there are a multitude of anxious eyes, squinting in the hot sun and from the exhaust clogged pit area, following those cars, experiencing the identical high pitched feeling and expectations of the skilled driver.

In the early fall, after sort of coasting around and casing the various business potentials, I bumped into Bob Hancock, and old high school chum and stock car driver from the jalopy days. He had raced at the Norfolk speedway in '48, driving a Ford, he had led the twenty five car field for thirty laps and would have gone on setting the pace had not the Ford lost its differential in the South turn. His car was a dead stick affair then, and he had bounced off the wall and into the path of an up and coming young driver named, Rudy Lock.

The Ford coupe was rapped again by a sliding Plymouth and in the hassle that followed, Bob had suffered spinal injuries. Although he walked slightly hunched, the accident hadn't slowed him down any.

His knowledge of car preparation rivaled that of the Spook and Elmer. Due to his wife's insistence, he no longer actively participated in driving, but a car was always entered in some event or another with Hancock backing.

He had informed me that he had moved to Morgantown from his former home in Polson, as his Ford dealership there was monopolized by larger dealers. His small agency couldn't match their ridiculous "deals" and he was forced to sell out. Upon settling in Morgantown, he had established himself as a Dodge dealer. Their excellent record on the track dept the coveted sales figure in the black.

We had conversed long that morning of the ailing Hornets the engine revolution, Morgantown's new mile track, and the return of some independents to the circuit among them, a red Dodge Ram with number 30 painted meticulously on its shining side!

My stagnant blood of past weeks of despair and indecision suddenly roared and pounded in my ears. The mere suggestion that he was racing again on his beloved circuit injected new life into my system. The image of that pale, determined individual was before me. I saw the squat Hornets in complete domination of the track, the Spook leading. The "magic hands" correcting for a four wheel drift, dropping a gear, accelerating, shifting to top gear. He was there. He was there as he always had been and the picture was vivid and real!

Bob interrupted my reverie with an invitation that Marty and I be his guests for dinner. He had stated that he had a business proposition, concerning his dealership and competition cars that might be interested in discussing!

Oh, what an elated man it was, who greeted his pert wife that afternoon. I hoisted her feather weight off the floor and swung her round and round. My feelings must have been contagious, for as I wheeled Marty through the living room and into her spotless kitchen, she smiled that smile that only a man's wife can.

What manner of a man was it that gave me that elation, for it was more the news of the Spook than Bob's hint of a team manager position that wiped the cobwebs from my head? Surely I was happy before I knew that he was somewhere back on the circuit. Marty was all the happiness that one could ever want or need. But, then it was something else again, when that slim figure came to mind, something of a challenge perhaps, a very different sort of person and the risk and uncertainty that revolved around him.

I realized then, how much, that he did mean to me. Someday...somewhere...we all meet out earthly master...I had met mine!

Then the withdrawal by the big fellas! Although I suspected the move just to be a lull. Let them all get out, Olds, Dodge and all the rest, and leave the racing to those that discovered it...the independents.

Good drivers, who previously could not afford to fight the inexhaustible resources and technical crews of the Detroit Barons, would now have an opportunity to demonstrate their prowess.

Bob and I glanced through the Tri-State Racing Journal, while Marty prepared dinner. Splashed on the front page was an Olds Rocket, number 61, and a number 30 Dodge entangled in a corner at a meet over near Polson. So Rudy and the Spook were at it again. Miss Mary came to mind and I wondered if the shining eyes were still glowing with love for the Spook.

Bob shook his head, "those two will be hard to beat, Bill."

"You're not kidding, they will. The Spook can't be beaten if he has a good mount under him. I don't give a damn, he just can't be beaten."

I wanted to make the point clear to Bob, so he wouldn't have any misgivings about jumping a new team in and acing the Spook and Rudy out of their familiar front running spots. The delicious thought of the Spook driving for us came to mind, but was put doubtfully aside. He would be content in the realm of independence for as long as the factories lay low. Olds was the only factory still backing dealers, the others mysteriously dropping out. What had happened? Didn't they realize sufficient sales increases since they dealt themselves a hand in this, the most hectic gamble ever? Maybe they were preparing for an onslaught at a later date. Whatever their reasons for disappearing…good riddance.

I mentioned the puzzling action to Bob who only shrugged and said, "If the factories return, we'll be here."

Such an optimistic statement! I understood factory domination only too well. When aid was terminated to us by the Hudson factory as the Hornets failed, we couldn't compete on a financial basis, instead were forced to disband.

"Down with those dour, defeating thoughts" I said. We were

going to have a stable of winners once more. I asked Bob if he had any drivers in mind and he replied with a negative movement of his head, whereas I suggested Buck and the boys from Norfolk.

"You're ramrodding the team Bill. Get whoever you think can put us out front."

We came to an agreement on salary that evening and a hand-someone it was to be.

As I drove home that evening, Marty snuggled up against me; I wondered when we might see him again. Judging by the Racing Journal, it was obvious that he was again making stock car history. Was the terrible force still driving him on and on, or had Miss Mary at least quieted it some? The big Olds driver was running an even closer second to the Spook. Had Rudy actually given up Miss Mary so easily? I looked for the bitter rivalry between that big bluff and the Spook to increase with each event, until either one, or both had been destroyed. You've heard that much used, worn-out saying used in western plays, "This here town ain't big enough for the two of us!" I doubted if the circuit was big enough for the incredible Spook and the treacherous Rudy Lock.

As if reading my thoughts, Mart asked, "What do you suppose Mary is doing? She hasn't written since we left Norfolk." Mart went on. "You know, Bill, I hope she stays away from that Spooky character and goes back with Rudy."

"Why on earth for Mart?"

"I've thought about it a lot, Bill, but I can't put my finger on it…not quite. There is something awfully strange about that man though…almost frightening!"

So she had felt the sinister feeling that revolved around him, too. Strongly enough to mention it out of the blue like that.

How could one man shape the lives of so many? He was just

as sure as I'm telling you this story. Would I not be a contented Hudson dealer in Norfolk had I not met him? Would not Miss Mary be engaged, or perhaps married to the red-faced Rudy by now had not that pallid, soft stepping figure interfered? What of Marty? For the first time in her life she was troubled by dark thoughts.

"Oh Bill, stop the car" she sobbed.

I jammed the brakes on, sliding to a halt on the gravel shoulder of the highway.

"Mart, what is it? What is it honey?" Her warm tears flowed down my hand like a little girl afraid of the future.

"It's going to be all right now Mart. Things are looking up now. Please don't cry Mart. Please don't"

What I took to be the release of tensions from the past few weeks of indecision turned out to be an entirely different matter. Marty was afraid of the Spook! Can you get that? Sure, he was the rarest and had given me the willies on occasions too.

"Hell Mart, he's on our side. You don't have to be afraid of him. Come on now."

"Something terrible is going to happen Bill, and Mary is going to be hurt. It's him Bill, can't you see?"

C'mon, Mart. Mary's going to straighten everything out for him. She's his answer. He needs her just like I need you doll, so dry the tears. It's going to be fine."

Mart began crying again as I pulled back onto the highway. All the elation of the day's events went sour in my mouth and I wondered if there was anything to her dreads of the future, concerning the Spook.

Only hours ago, he had given me sheer joy and now he was taking it back without even being present....or was he...?

The Hornets of various other teams throughout the country were slowly going under, although in the main division of the vast coverage of the Association and its affiliates, a Hudson driver finished second in national point standings. The Spook, Rudy, and a well liked and respected family man, battled for first point rating in our division.

Wielding a huge, dun-colored Chrysler, Lee Petty was a consistent threat to the Spook and Rudy in their private warfare.

The thickest clouds of battle hung over the small, dealer-sponsored groups of Dodge and Olds, and just when all expectations had arisen for the same makes to storm away on the 1955 circuit, a new undisputed champion arose. Yes, a trend began then, that was to continue for years to come. The first of the super stocks made its debut, the Chrysler 300!

Patterned after their successful 331-inch engine, the Chrysler Corporation followed the example of the hot rodders and brought out a power plant that sported not less than 300 stampeding ponies. The chassis was constructed to handle the hurricane power of that ferocious heavyweight unleashed, the thundering 300's promptly steamrolling to one victory after another. The beauty of the cars was that the taxi driver, barber, grocer, the enthusiast in any walk of life could truthfully stop in at a Chrysler dealer and order themselves a genuine "stock car" right off the showroom floor!

1955 will be the year too that we will all remember the big man from Wisconsin and his team of 300's. Not since our record smashing performance records of Carl Keikhaefer and his fabulous, big, white cars.

Dominating the large purse events of that year, The Chrysler 5 finished 1-2-3 repeatedly and at the insistence of the frustrated losers, were completely dismantled and checked for unfair modifications at the end of several races, at which time they were found to be as disgustingly stock as a 300 horsepower engine can be!

Marty and Bob's wife Ellen were palling around a lot together since Bob and I had become associated, and with their meandering here and there, they came across a ranch-style house somewhat resembling Bob and Ellen's.

Marty spoke to me concerning the property one evening at supper, enthusiasm showing brightly in her face. The place we were occupying at the time was convenient and all, but left much to be desired from a women's standpoint.

We had rented the building with an option, so were not under any obligation to remain, should we choose to move.

Marty was bubbling over so on the subject of the new place that we had decided to go out that following weekend and case the situation.

The house sat resolutely on a high point of ground, an immense yard surrounding it. I parked the company Dodge and Mart and I walked up the long ribbon-like path to the front porch.

We were admitted by an elderly woman, who explained that the place belonged to her son and daughter-in-law and, further, that they were out of town at the time and could not be reached. The property was for sale, however, and we were welcome to look around.

What a layout! Everything was on one floor. None of that up and down jazz that we had at our present residence.

A monstrous, modern kitchen set off by a floor so highly polished that it stung the eyes with its reflection. I nudged Mart and said, "What a slick dog." The floor wasn't even a trifle slippery and she made me eat the words.

There was a living room large enough for the whole team with a couple of trucks thrown in. Real plush furniture, with all kinds of little rugs here and there. Of course, the fireplace was what caught my attention.

I enjoyed assembling a group together for a marshmallow roast, with all the house lights turned out and only the flickering tongues of flame dancing around on everyone's flushed faces.

There was a play room for kids and one for the old man. The latter was referred to as a den, and Marty snickered behind my back. She always called me an old lion whenever I was sore, so I guess that the den title would be appropriate.

There was a rumpus room with all the necessities for a real stormer party, also with a fireplace. I don't know yet how many bedrooms the joint had, but there were at least a dozen sprinkled from one end to the other of the lengthy hallway.

"Well Mart, if we're going to splurge…..zis is zee place" I kidded her.

I contacted the owner, a Mister Myers, later in the week and we dickered back and forth for the better part of a day, finally coming to terms.

"Whoosh!" That's all I could say at the signing of the contract. I would be paying for that castle until the heaven boys called up my number, or the jokers employed downstairs as coal shovelers.

"What the hell" I said. Business was on the upswing all over the nation and I was always sure of a place with Bob for as long as he had one himself. Besides, if everything went well, we could have the place paid for in say twenty years! My Mart had her house though, and I could hardly wait to tell her the deal was sealed.

We did throw that party too. By the following Saturday, we

had moved into our "castle" as Mart called it, and began mailing out housewarming invites to everyone we could think of. We sent an invitation to the Spook via the Tri-State Racing Journal.

I wrote a letter to Nick and told him to close up the Note and bring along a few cases of that damn Scotch of his. He would do it too. Next to bragging up his Scotch, there was nothing he liked better than sampling same in a real down to hell party.

Mart invited some single gals from town because there would be more males otherwise as with all parties I had ever attended.

Buck was married, but Pat and Jerry were single and always open for suggestion. Mary naturally was invited and would probably drive up, spending the night with us. Mary had become an exceptional driver since her instruction by the Spook, and was getting sharp with the downshifts.

Mary showed up the afternoon prior to the party and came charging into the yard in a bright red '55 Plymouth. The little engine really revved up and had a set of dual exhaust with a sound all its own.

I asked her why she had bought a red Plymouth and she answered that a friend had picked the car out for her. Yes, I could imagine what friend all right.

Mary and Mart busied themselves in preparation for the "main event" as we referred to it, while I took stock of the liquor supply.

There appeared to be sufficient quantity of the "glow fluid" especially if Nick brought his Scotch. Those drivers were a thirsty lot though, so I went into Morgantown to pick up a few more bottles.

They came from all corners of our Tri-State area. Big ones, little ones, tall ones and skinny ones. Our driveway resembles the pits on race day, with every make represented. There were bound to be technical arguments that night and I made mental note to appoint a bouncer.

Three yellow Olds arrived about midnight, Rudy and his bunch making an appearance. I hadn't invited the character, but supposed Mart did. I couldn't ignore him as long as he was there, so I stumbled out front and let the "noise" in.

"Hi Nordic," he smirked. "I figured you forgot to invite me, so just came along anyway."

"Uh huh" I replied, staring at the assuming man with glassy, blank eyes.

As the coo-coo clock struck three, a couple of guys crawled in, carrying two big, wooden boxes. Swaying on his feet, Nick Sitell stood a short distance behind them, his hat cocked at a jaunty, playboy angle. He apologized for bringing only the two cases, but explained that there had been three.

"Ish waz aaaa long tripps up shere, Billy boy."

"Yah Nick, I know." How in the hell they had ever made it was beyond me.

"Whooopeee!" Nick grabbed some doll that was sauntering by, near mauling her in an intoxicated attempt to dance. She cussed him as she fell to the floor, Nick on top and laughing like a born clown. She swatted him half a dozen times and ran into the next room.

Nick staggered to his feet and swung at her, but his depth perception was somewhat amiss because she had already disappeared.

I helped him get reoriented with himself and pointed him the general direction of the bar.

A ruckus developed in one of the side rooms, and I rushed on the scene in time to see Rudy deck Curtis Turner, a Ford driver, with a smashing right. Rudy was ranting something about the Olds being top car, swinging his hulking frame in a wide arc. Upon attempting to calm the big Rocket driver down, he made a pass at me, nearly connecting.

He was setting himself up for another, when a cool, steady voice asked from behind, "Need a bouncer Bill?"

Rudy stood still as death, gazing at the Spook. I asked Rudy if he thought I needed a bouncer, but he didn't answer. I thought for a moment he was going to fight the Spook, but apparently the slashing blows dealt him on his first attempt were still imprinted on his booze clouded mind.

Their gazes held for a few seconds more, but Rudy's finally dropped under that driving force of the terrible eyes and he retreated into the dimness of the rumpus room to nurse his injured pride over a drink.

Miss Mary came into the front room, her eyes immediately fastening on those of the Spook. They had their silent conversation for a short time and eventually, arm in arm they left.

I watched them move away together, then went to close the front door as a silent wind whispered across my neck....The door was already closed....

The lull was broken...The factories appeared with all their might for the '56 season. All the manufacturers had racing budgets comparable to the Grand Prix teams of Europe prior to the Second World War

Never before had the circuit seen such incredible speeds and performance. The pits were packed with highly efficient people and their factory sponsored drivers.

I doubted that even the glowing green eyes could quell that

terrible fire that was bound to be aggravated by such a robust challenge set forth by the Barons of Detroit...

As the season progressed, the independents became hopelessly outclassed. Factory support was a necessity. What little sentimentality we had regained with the factory absence was more than lost upon their return, and our Tri-State circuit turned back into the gnashing nightmare growing worse with every restless contest.

At this point, it is interesting, and perhaps a little sorrowing, to note that the Keikhafer stable of the Chrysler 300's received no financial aid from the Chrysler factory, although technical advice was given them on occasions.

That great man from Wisconsin, even though winning the majority of large purse events, must have been spending a tremendous amount of his own money on his championship cars and drivers.

Unlike some of the other major racing organizations, who still raced exclusively on the oval and circle tracks, Tri-State with the exception of the 500 milers, sponsored all road races in the 1956 season.

Possibly, the reason for this was that the public cried for the stockers on the road courses. Again, too, it may have been that with the advent of all super stocks they felt a road course would be most exciting for the spectators. Bob and I felt that Detroit was behind the action, speculating on how the cars would hold up under the twisting stress of the many sharp turns and serpentines of such a course.

We were all for it. Besides, that's how cars were constructed to go. Not in the continuous circle, that often became boring to some of the less enthusiastic, when one or two cars led the field by one or two laps, gaining steadily.

Give up the road race and a covey of various makes of cars, winding through a series of esses!

The Spook, as an independent entry, came onto the racing scene just as it was getting into full swing. The factories had been watching for him and I'll wager every representative from the millionaire teams had asked him for his able and tireless skills. I was sure he would fall into one of the organizations, possibly Ford, which had an almost unlimited budget for the season.

He would have too, but the Ford man sent to speak with him didn't actually ask him, but made his question more or less an ultimatum.

"You either drive for us, or we'll wreck you." I don't know if those were the man's words or not, but they insinuated as much, from what I could gather from an office girlfriend of Marty's.

There was no sense me prodding him any, as he knew he had a place with us anytime. We wanted him as a driver sure, but also as a remarkable individual, who would be an inspiration to the other drivers.

Understanding the Spook better than anyone, except Mary, and aware of that uncontrollable fire inside him, that demanded his all and thrust him forward at a merciless pace, I knew that he would be forced to establish himself as the utmost, the superior driver, among the new crop of great talents that arose with the super stocks. Call it vanity, pride if you choose, but we, you and I, know that it was something far removed from any critic's conception. We know that it was the white, hot, burning torch inside him, so intense that it showed outwardly as the terrible eyes and the driving force and had to be further released in the fury and risk of the race, lest it grow inside him and destroy him. The Spook....

I was again reminded of our own victorious crew of Hudson's, Pat, Jerry, Buck and him the Spook. I had thought it would be very appropriate to see the Spook driving on the Keikhaefer team, but he never made an appearance with them.

Bob Hancock was a man who possessed much foresight, both in everyday activities and in situations pertaining to the future. Our Red Ram Dodge were doing well on the shorter tracks but weren't finishing at the top of the heap as planned. Bob had felt, with the appearance of the mighty 300's, other superstocks would soon be in production, Dodge among them. He decided to race the red Rams another season, with the knowledge that we could never catch the 300's, but could hold down the Olds and the few remaining Hornets, insuring us at least a breakeven point, financially.

The competition was terrific, not from the standpoint of speed so much, as traffic. The tracks were cluttered with cars, the collision danger a constant menace, especially with the advent of new, green drivers. Young guys anxious to make a name for themselves on the circuit.

With an over abundance of nerve and lack of skill and experience, the accident rate rose. One youth, undoubtedly inspired by the Spook, had the numbers 30 painted on his rickety, old Plymouth, until the Association informed him that those previous numbers were already registered to another driver. What a rat race!

The Association eventually ruled that all green drivers start at the back of the field and do no more than maintain their starting positions, until their driving could be improved by actual experience so necessary for cars that were steadily becoming faster and faster.

That ruling worked fine to an extent, but there were still too many cars at an event for the size of the tracks themselves.

Shortly, another ruling was put forth, limiting the number of cars per contest. The latter law achieved the much sought after results and we were able to continue as before, the pace growing swifter with each meet.

A portion of the youths that were left out by the Association ruling seemed bitter. The ever vigilant group at headquarters remedied this factor by establishing additional contests.

The amateur division was exploited, new drivers appearing in droves. The old pros were beside themselves with frustration.

"Racing's too hot of a business to have a bunch of green kids around." They had remarked.

"But, it was also a free country, and the "apprentices," as they were referred to dept coming.

I recall instances, when the Spook was racing the number 30 Hornet, when the track was crowded, factory entries all over the place. He had shaken his head in what seemed like disgust, and had commenced to hurl the Hudson through traffic like it was a toy, instead of a full-sized car, winning the event of 2 full laps on Pat and Rudy Lock.

There had been eight contenders out because of wrecks, six of which had been sent ingloriously through the fence, after being prodded in the corners by a sliding number 30 Hornet.

Pat Polotel, and official starter for the Association, had informed me that he had been asked by the Trison sports car club to be flagman for one of their rallies at the road course, near Morgantown. He had taken the job after receiving permission from the Association. He was positive he had seen the Spook, driving one of the tiny racers.

"Has he gone over to sports cars, Bill?"

"I don't know Pat, I don't know." I knew the Spook had always favored the small sports car because of their fine handling and overall performance.

Sports car racing in our area was limited to amateur competitors at that time, and there were no purses or any form of prize money. I couldn't quite figure the Spook racing for free, unless he was just keeping in form and wasn't after the money side of the picture. Pat said that he had really gone down the road! Tooling a new Chevy Corvette, he had out driven two well-known sports car men in superior Mercedes machines and won first place in his class.

That sounded like him all right, but was he going to stay away from the stocks for good?

Knowing his devotion to the beefed up Detroiters and with traffic thinning down, I looked forward to witnessing the legendary 30 in running once more.

— — — — — — — — — — —

Spurred by the highly successful Chrysler 300, other super stocks began to appear. Plymouth produced the "Fury" model that was capable of 140 miles an hour in "stock" configuration. The competition model, with additional carburetion and wicked camshaft, could hold its own against its thundering big brother, the Chrysler 300-B, which had already established itself as speed king, hitting over 160 miles per in the flying mile tests at Daytona Beach Speed Weeks.

Ford, discarding their 1955 selling point, safety, produced the "Interceptor." Chevy, top car on the short tracks in '55 was doing remarkably well with a light, fast, high-revving V-8 of relatively small displacement.

I would grit my teeth in expectation of a blown engine, every time a Chevy sped by the pits. I felt that the four quart capacity of their oil system was rather inadequate for such screaming revs. I was disproved at every race, as the little mills stayed in one piece as well as any of the super cars did.

Our own Dodge gave us the impressive D-500 engine, and later on in the '56 conflict brought out an even hotter version, designated as the D-501. With improved manifolding and camming, the 501's horsepower rating was a muscular 275, compared to 260 of the straight 500. Either "bomb" would slash eight seconds in a 0 to 60 acceleration test.

Again, Bob's foresight had paid off, our not too sensational '54 red Rams bowing to the successors, the confident 501's.

The Olds though still placing well, found themselves in the same position that the Nordic and Clark Hornets had encountered only two years previously, and were falling on poor tunes against the thundering 300's, Ford's Interceptor, the screeching Chevy's and our sweet, potent 501's.

Plymouth's Fury model, though certainly no slouch on any track, ever seemed to live up to what was expected of them, because of so few entries. Unlike their counterpart, the 501, the Fury's racing package was not so readily available. Our 500 models, that we used before the Association recognized the 501, has done well, racing on a plane with Ford's 260 horse Interceptors and Chevy's high revving 225 horses. That was on the shorter courses. On the Grand National scene, it was all the 300'Bs the Keikhafer Corporation winning sixteen straight victories, repeating their

'55 procedure. We were confident that the 501's would upset them through and we all worked feverishly in their preparation.

Bob and I, upon completing our office work, meandered out into Elmer's undisputed domain of the shop. The thoroughness with which the "stock cars" were "set up" was outstanding. Bob and I watched in awe, as every movement by Elmer and his assistants was accounted for.

To begin with, the engines were completely disassembled and dynamically balanced for perfection. Elmer discarded many pistons before finding eight that matched accurately in weight and quality. Precision-fitted, though looser than ordinary highway driving, yet snug enough to prevent slapping and excessive wear. An extra engine mount was added at the front because of the abuse administered by the tracks. Alterations to the water pump were performed in order to slow up the flow of that previous liquid.

An assembled engine, checked out on the Dynamometer failed to perform satisfactorily, Elmer ordering a complete dismantling, puckering his lips in contemplation as to the nature of the trouble. We usually ran an engine two races, depending on the conditions raced under, then Elmer completely rebuilt them again. We weren't fooling, we were out to win!

If you are an enthusiast, and doubtlessly you are, or you wouldn't have read this far, you will be interested in the painstaking labor put in on a chassis "set up."

The bodies were unbolted from the chassis and dropped over in the comer of the shop, several aggressive young mechanics swarming over the naked steel of the long frame.

One kid begins work on the car's exhaust system, which in finished form will sport new three-inch diameter pipes, terminating slightly to the rear of the doors and ahead of the rear-wheels. An unrestricted exhaust flow is essential to engine life, especially there, on the pounding of the circuit.

A fuel tank is wrapped in spun glass to better keep gasoline temperatures constant, lessening the chance of vapor locking, thus starving the engine of its power.

An anti-sway bar is added along the rear axle to give more stability.

Two shock absorbers, of a heavy duty type, are installed at each wheel and are adjustable to suit the characteristics of various racing surfaces. Coil springs, one would expect to see on a pick-up truck, are used on the front end while on the rear spring set up, extra leaves are used to follow the pattern of the "beefing up" procedure. Brake cooling, a major problem of racing, is taken care of to a certain degree by the ventilation of the brake drums with fine, wire screens.

Brake drums are also drilled at an angle to scoop the valuable cooling air, rushing past the churning wheels. A special ceramic, bronze-base lining is welded to the brake shoe, the steel return spring able to withstand two and a half times more heat than normal. A primary concern with the racers, brakes receive the pampering of a newborn kitten in a house full of kids.

An air intake hose stretches from the outside of the car and down to the brake drum itself.

The body exterior shell that hides so many mechanical won-ders is dealt a touch of treatment, too.

Doors are bolted shut for obvious safety reasons, and other chrome decorations are peeled off to lessen wind resistance at high speed, the unlovely holes left by its absence filled in with a lead compound, later to be covered by the team racing colors and a portion of the car's number.

Pat Jensen shakes with expectation as he moves about his 22 car, released by the technical division of the shop and in the hands of the agile group, assigned to cockpit preparation, a division devoted solely to the purpose of the machine's interior, such as the stout rollover bar spreading over the roof of the 501, seatbelts and shoulder harnesses, removing unwanted accessories from the Detroit cluttered dashboard, and driver convenience and comfort, Seats are built up to suit the driver, for the long, sapping grind of a 500 miler takes its toll in sweat and nerves.

All these things that I have mentioned are only a small part of what goes into a championship car, so you see it takes top mechanics too, to win races. Without the skill and patience of the men in the shop, the high strung, lightning-reflexed driver wouldn't even leave the ground. It takes both and we were lucky to have them. I only wished he, the Spook, could have been there, his magic hands improving on some innovation of a lesser man.

Confident that the Spook would not appear from the Ford team, I thought we might see him in one of the big Keikhaefer 300's. He hadn't driven for them on the '55 circuit, so the only other alternatives he had were the Chevys, Plymouths, or us unless of course he was going to compete within some other organization.

Olds was a doubtless possibility, what with Rudy Lock still on their payroll. Surely he wouldn't fight them as an independent… or would he?

The Association had decided to run a 350-miler, in order to adjust their schedule, on Morgantown's new completed track.

That was when the Spook came back on the racing scene,

driving that same '54 Dodge of course, number 30. What remote chance did the outdated red Ram have against the super stocks?

The Ford team, determined to destroy him closed in three cars strong on the south turn. It was on lap 150, and the red Dodge, suffering from ignition trouble, was stuttering through the corner. Apparently, the Spook must have advanced the timing to give him just a little more blast out of the turns. As was customary, a car in trouble pulled to the right side of the track. This he did, but the boys in the purple cars wouldn't let him be, instead one bumping him in the rear, another slamming him on the side.

As the Dodge began swaying and swinging toward the wall, the Ford pilots broke away, thinking they had eliminated him.

He came close to losing the tired, protesting Dodge, but as if receiving a boost from some unseen element, the small V-8 hemi caught a shot of juice, accelerating after its adversaries.

He couldn't catch the swift Interceptors on the straight but lo and behold, that same turn, four laps later, when the red 30, guided by that still, vapor-like figure, annihilated two of his antagonists by extremely unorthodox methods. The event had nearly developed into one of the old destruction derbies of past years.

The Association called all the men involved down on the incident, but with their new forced laxity at headquarters, no one was fined or suspended.

In slam bang fashion, simple for anyone to comprehend, he had let them know he was not to be fooled with.

It was evident that the red Ram, fine, competitive car it had been, could not hope to accomplish the impossible. The Spook realized this fact, but had to call the Ford representatives bluff first.

He stopped by the shop one day where we discussed the preceding race. The old, icy exterior was plain and I wished for Mary's presence, so that I might speak with the pleasant, educated man that was the Spook's quiet side when soothed first by the emerald eyes of Miss Mary.

I asked him if he had driven any of the super stocks yet and he replied negatively. We looked over the dual quad carburetion manifolding of a customer's 501, and decided to take a spin.

I recognized the car as belonging to a Chuck Swensen, an old Swede, who had purchased the Dodge only a month previous, after witnessing the impressive show put on by Buck and the boys on the last road race.

Having formerly driven a six cylinder car of miniature displacement around town, he had constantly complained of the thirsty gas mileage of the 326 cubic inch 501. I guess he figured if he operated the engine at slower RPM, he would increase his mileage. The 501's weren't exactly designed to turn over at ridiculously low revs, Chuck's pampered Dodge turning into a congested, asthmatic old sludge pot, that smoked worse that a worn-out stocker.

At any rate, he had been bringing the car in every other day for a tune-up.

Old Swensen had ordered a conventional shift transmission in the car, and it was this the Spook nodded in approval. I prepared myself for what I thought was to be an adventure on wheels.

Heads turned toward the shop from all up and down Eighth Street.

Bob Hancock's heavy-jowled features formed into a wide smile as the Spook wound the swelling voice of the 501 to fifty miles plus in first gear and an instantaneous shift to second, accompanied by the squeal of astonished rear tires. Swensen stared in disbelief from the interior of his store on Filbert Street as we breezed past.

Oh Lord, I thought. How would I explain this one?

I figured to tell him that we were checking his car for cutout in the ignition system. Of course he wouldn't know what I was talking about anyway, but wouldn't care to admit his ignorance in the matter, I could just picture him, wagging his head in false intelligence, a puzzled frown clouding his forehead. He would never be able to fathom the way with which his Dodge shot away.

The Spook stopped for a safety walk, two pedestrians waddling across the street, unaware of the car and the man that were as one. He, the Spook suggested that we take a run out the old Colton River Highway, which with the opening of the Colton Freeway, was used only on occasions by sightseeing tours from Norfolk.

The road was a real challenge and we had thought of establishing it as a course, but due to its poor location, rough surface and insufficient capacity for spectator safety, the Association had vetoed the idea. It was splendid for practice though, and we frequently brought the team there for trial runs. Located in the foothills of the Colton Range, the road had some sweet, banked turns.

After fueling at Barney's station, we left the freeway and began to ascend into the Colton's, the 501 gulping in the fresh, clean mountain air.

The stock suspension system on the 501 was very rigid, presenting a firm, stable ride.

The Spook shook his head in disdain at the slow action of the manual steering, which required four turns from lock to lock. A "stocker" conditioned for the track usually was a mere three turns or less.

As on many of the old, twisting highways, the Colton employed indicated safe speed signs on the curves.

"Lord," I had mused aloud, as the Spook hurled the Dodge at 80, through a bend stipulating 45 MPH. With the absence of traffic, he started into the turns on the extreme left hand side of the highway, negotiating an accurate and exact four-wheel drift, his pale expression never altering.

I felt my own visage grow red, then white, not because I wavered in my opinion of the master at the controls, but because my poor stomach swayed from side to side as the clamoring 501 streaked through the esses like a fugitive projectile! We had been bearing down, rather at a frightful rate, on a hairpin curve, marked 25. The Spook upon shifting to third gear on a gradual left hand bend, was still accelerating, the speedometer indicating a disaster 75.

With slightly over one hundred feet to the turn, he removed his heavy foot from the gas pedal, tapping the superb Dodge brakes twice, harder the second time. He dropped into second gear and braked hard at the same time. We were in the turn! His hand flashed on the column gearshift lever and we were magically in first gear, powering out of the hairpin, the front wheels turned slightly to correct for the rear end slide. Feathering the throttle, the Spook hastened the car through the turn magnificently. He slammed the 501 into second at fifty, wound the healthy sounding mill up to 65, and eased the Dodge to the summit.

Where the biggest thrill came in was on the descent. I wake at night marveling of it yet.

The Spook had been allowing for the slower steering characteristics of Chuck's Dodge and everything would have gone fine, had not one of the sightseeing busses chosen that particular day to come around a blind corner, in the center of the highway! The curve was another left hand turn and was obscured by thick undergrowth. The sign post had a bright 30MPH suggested for the Sunday drivers and I guess the terrible eyes must have fastened on that glorious number longer than he had intended them to.

Well, we were nearly in the corner and still doing 60 in second gear. I think he was planning on braking to 50 then if the way was clear, cutting into the left lane and slide through the turn. We would have come out of the turn superbly, in a slight rear end drift, but there was that bus,…astraddle the white line….

What happened next was a little out of my class, even to explain. That fantastic individual, in all his splendor, was in his element. The risk, chance and uncertainty were there and he accepted them without hesitation, his reflexes that were three times that of an ordinary man, responded with blurring speed too swift for the eye to follow!

He reefed the Dodge to the right, in order to miss the loaded bus, and we began to "swap ends." I had figured that was it, we had had it, and looked over at him, naked fear mirrored in my face. He was grinning…can you imagine that….grinning like a skunk at a picnic!

There we were, aboard a panicked machine, surely scheduled for the 100 foot precipice that yawned so invitingly up at us and he was bubbling over with joy. Not this kid…I was praying harder than I ever had before!

The 501 did swap ends, but the Spook was the employer, the Dodge; the wage earner, and he steered through the dangerous situation, undaunted and unafraid. We made the complete 360 heading in our original direction.

"Whoosh," is all I could think of to say as I shrank down in my seat from sheer relief. The smile left his lips and he was content the remainder of the journey to the shop, not once exceeding 100 MPH.

We returned the 501 to Elmer, who puckered up his lips upon feeling the temperature of the tires.

The Spook claimed that he liked the Dodge accepting my offer to drive on the team.

Oh, but I was proud to have him with us again. I was somewhat doubtful how Marty would accept the news, but I would explain to her how we needed his unequaled prowess to break through into the winning spots again.

Chuck Swensen picked up his "tuned up" 501 and never complained of the machine running sour again...

— — — — — — — — — — —

So it was that our long awaited 500-miler, climaxing the season, came to be. Morgantown was filled with cars and drivers from all over the country. The multitude had been growing with each passing day and I doubted there would be room for all those eager spectators, even with the tremendous capacity of our new speedway.

At the shop0, the 501's had priority on all customers, Elmer, George and their staff of assistants laboring feverishly to have the cars in peak condition for the much sought after victory, concluding the long conflicting season.

Our entire organization, from office girl to competition driver, were wound clear to the top. This was racing. Past differences had been forgotten, petty squabbles dismissed. Vance Marlow, shirt sleeves rolled up and paint brush in hand, was touching up the numerals on the freshly washed cars. I slapped him on the shoulder as I passed. We were, without question, a winning team!

The pessimistic Elmer supervised one last engine check, frowning, listening intently down to the very soul of the roaring 501. Seemingly satisfied, he unpuckered his lips and nodded at his mechanics. Hoods came down and were securely fastened shut with safety wire.

Pickup trucks backed into the shop and fastened tow bars to the shimmering racers. We locked up at ten o'clock, everyone heading for the speedway to witness the last battle of a long, turbulent season!

If you have ever attended one of the major races, you will understand the feeling that we were all experiencing. The festive yet high pitched tension in the air. Bystanders discussing and arguing, with an authority that would abash the most technical expert. One man says "My car's the best." Another counters with, "No, mine is!" A woman enthusiast spits, "You're both crazy. My car has won the most races!" The two men smirk, then join sides against the new antagonist... On and on they go, more angry voices chiming in, until only the race itself will decide the issue. Propping themselves against the fence, waiting for the gates to open, a group of well-dressed men make wagers, their faces keen and calculating, as they watch our small procession wind its way through the slow traffic.

A flurry of jeers follow us from some intoxicated critics of the Dodge.

A Chevy supporter yells, "Where are you taking those klunks?... The wrecking yard's that way!" Bob makes motion to get out of the car and the bantering fellow dissipates into the crowd.

Someone hollers, "There go the winning cars," and Bob and I grin at one another. Then we are away from the ceaseless turmoil of the crowd, and into the familiar turmoil of our own kind.

Cars, fresh with new paint, line the pit area. Factory names are loudly displayed at their respective pits. Thousands of dollars worth of spare parts and extra cars clog the runway.

Two tow trucks were on hand, and two ambulances, complete with doctors and attendants. The Association was expecting some mishaps!

Our number 30 came onto the track. He looked worse than I had ever seen him, his face actually faint, almost as though there was no one inside the white uniform that clothed his thin, emaciated frame.

"You know Doc, I'm glad I had that examination last week and it's finished with. I dislike this medical rigmarole," the Spook told Doc Toner.

Doc made not reply, but held his head low, broodingly. There had been that mistake and "the boys" were being mislead more and more by those contemptible engines.

"I quit the circuit for several months, Doc. Mary was there with me all the time and she kept telling me I could stay away from the cars. I just did not deem it possible, but this season winds up my racing career. It's Mary…she…that is…well, we're going to be married after the 500-miler here at Norfolk. I'll be a mechanic after that, but no more driving."

Still, Doc Toner said nothing, his head sinking lower, his frown-burrowed brows and his ashen face a sight of utter defeat.

"Hey Doc, did you hear me?"

"Son"

"Spit it out Doc. Don't tell me I'm not the healthiest specimen you ever saw."

"Son." Doc paused again. "Your general health is run down, but could be improved…It's not that…it's…

His voice turned cold and the terrible eyes in evidence, the Spook asked, "What is it Doc, am I sick?

"The blood test son, it's the blood test."

"What about the blood test?"

"Spook, you have advanced leukemia!"

Silence prevailed as the sentencing statement seemed to repeat itself over and over, reverberating from the walls and from the ceiling of the tiny office.

The Spook walked to the window and stared across the highway, past the level farm lands, his piercing, glazed eyes dismissing the tall, pointed spires of the great Colton's and searching the vast infinite sky itself for a hint of the mysterious beyond.

"How long have I Doc?"

"If…if you will follow my instructions and stay away from the circuit…you may have a year Spook….My boy, I', so sorry." Doc arose, cross the distance separating them and laid a consoling hand on the Spook's arm.

For no clear reason, the Spook had broken everything off with Miss Mary. It didn't seem possible to any of us, particularly Mart and I, who knew better than most the ardent devotion between the two.

Mary had informed Mart that he had just told her, it was… too late!

When Mary had inquired what, where, when and the like, he had just gazed off into the distance, muttering, "goodbye Mary," and walked away, out of her life. Just when we were all beginning to understand that adept individual, he pulled a stunt like that. I didn't get it, but why should I worry about it? Was it my place to ponder another man's decisions?

Maybe he felt the circuit was no life to share with someone of Mary's temperament, and that she was going to ask him to make a choice between her and the speed that dictated his person. Whatever were his reasons, they were not my affair and I was going to close my mind to the whole puzzling business.

Mary's greenest of eyes, though still maintaining their stately sheen, had somehow looked clouded and bewildered.

"Oh, to hell with it," I had spat, tromping in the direction of one of the 501's.

The tranquility and contentment of past months that had been mirrored on his face disappeared, and in their place were the dreadful eyes and the driving force.

What in the hell could have gone wrong?

Despite himself, he could not conceal his impassioned feeling for Mary when she was near, although he avoided her completely, nearly to the extent of rudeness. I found myself resenting and condemning him for his stuffiness toward Mary, who was heartbroken and hurt. The least he could do was to explain to her.

Mary had spent considerable time at our place within the following weeks, trying to talk the pain away. It was no gook and each day she became thinner, her faint complexion matching that of the Spook's.

Rudy had learned of the situation and began to call, Mary at first rejecting him and continuing to brood and hang her head.

One afternoon, an Olds skidded to a lurching half in the drive, and a goliath figure emerged, bounding to the front door and ringing the bell impatiently. Knowing who was to gift us with his unwanted presence, I shrank down in my chair, closed my eyes, feigning sleep.

Marty knew me pretty well and tapped me on the shoulder saying, "We saw him drive up too Bill."

I opened my eyes to find her standing over me, hands on hips and a quizzical little smile playing at the corners of her mouth.

I grumbled a shallow oath making sure she didn't hear the words used, and rose from the comfort of my soft chair, walking to the door.

There he stood and I felt like slamming the heavy oak door right in that face full of teeth. Instead, I asked politely , with the knowledge that Marty was listening, "What can I do for you, Rudy?"

"I came to see Mary Nordic," he sneered sarcastically through his big, too white teeth.

"Why?" I had spat back curtly, only to hear a long, drawn out "Biiiilllll," from Marty. I was helpless under her close scrutiny, so I motioned Rudy inside, gesturing toward my own vacated chair.

He plopped his titanic frame down, crossed his thick legs and graced us with his favorite sneer, asking, "Has the creep learned to drive yet Nordic?"

There was no sense answering the clamorous man, so I planted a bold silent stare right on his smirking face.

Now anyone with an ounce of integrity or anything at all to them, would have wilted, or at least become embarrassed under such an obviously hateful glare.

Rudy? His face became redder, his teeth grew bigger and whiter and his brashness literally drove me to violence. If Marty hadn't been there…! The sweat of nervous tension began to prickle my forehead and I thought someone had better come to my rescue, or so help me....

Mary came in from the hallway and asked, "What is it Rudy?"

"How would you like to come on a drive with me, say, over the Coltons?" His rashness and smirk disappeared up on addressing Mary.

I don't know if she had done it to rescue us, or because she was tired of staying put in the house, but she looked at Mart, a question in the green troubled eyes. Marty nodded at her.

"Why not? I'll be ready in a minute. Bill will keep you entertained, won't you, Bill?" She teased, that same way Marty had, when the unrestrained man had first arrived.

Well, if nothing else was accomplished by going with Rudy, maybe she would regain some color to her face, that had become almost as wan as the Spook's.

Dogs, cats, old ladies and kids scattered, as the yellow Olds laid forty feet of rubber upon leaving the driveway. He just wouldn't be Rudy Lock, unless he displayed an act like that.

I hoped Mary knew what she was doing, going with a fizzle like him. It didn't seem possible that she had ever been associated with the man at all. It somehow seemed as though she and the Spook had always been together. If only the gap between them could be filled, and he could subdue that awful turbulence that drove him incessantly, and too, discard that dark outlook that compelled him to think it was too late...

Why didn't I have enough sense than to see what was happening? Although it's difficult to write about, let alone believe, the Spook's driving began to falter! He was spinning the powerful 501 out a dozen times in a contest. On the straights, nearly every

87

driver on the track was eluding him. I had seen men lose their self-confidence before and the Spook definitely showed those symptoms, much of his trouble, I had thought, was due to the fact that he seldom slept or even rested anymore, and of course, something beyond that, which made him split up with Mary. The factory was appalled by the losses we were being dealt by Chevy and Ford and came forth with an ultimatum.

Vance Marlow, representing Dodge's racing division, had witnessed the unbelievable actions of the Spook at an International rally on the Morgantown sports car course. An International race is where makes from various countries all compete in one big mix-up.

Vance had called Bob and me for a conference the following day. We had no misgivings as to what the topic of conversation was to center around, and speaking for myself, I felt somewhat upset. A natural, such as the Spook, doesn't lose his skill and ability, but may need and intermission from the hot grinding of the circuit.

With that thought in mind, Bob and I went in to face Vance Marlow from headquarters.

"Gentlemen," Vance began. "I have been instructed by the factory to inform you that you have a decision to make. Either your driver, this Spook, has to go or Dodge will terminate all support. I'm sorry to seem so blunt, but we have sat back for some time now witnessing his defeats at the hands of the most novice driver. We had contemplated that you, gentlemen would remedy the matter on your own initiative. Since you have taken no corrective measures, we find it necessary to step in on the matter. Naturally, we want to continue supporting your racing program, but of course, the decision lies with you. You understand, I take it, that Dodge has dealerships all over the Tri-State area, receiving financial backing and technical aid. When one such firm requires our advice, concerning drivers or equipment, we naturally recommend what we consider best for the company itself, and its product."

It had sounded more to me like a speech by a damn dictator. How the hell could the factory know what was best concerning the Spook? Sure, he had been dragging then, but hadn't he given them their biggest victories many times?

I told Marlow this and he replied instantly in his soft, smooth flowing voice.

"We realize the past performance of this man and greatly appreciate the fact that he has won with our cars on countless occasions, but...the fact remains that we have to protect our own interests too. As you gentlemen know, factory sponsorship in the stock car racing scene is taking place by all the major manufacturers. Thousands and thousands of dollars too are going into vast advertising campaigns, as to the results of the make or makes of car in question. To be blunt again...some of your recent results haven't given the factory much to advertise, unless we want to proclaim to all the car conscious people over the country, that a number 30 Dodge, hottest make in our line, finished twenty-eighth, in a thirty-two car field!

His smirk resembled that of Rudy Lock's, with those finishing words.

I could see panic plainly written on Bob's face and knew he had already made a decision, regarding the failing Spook. With a note of remorse in his voice, he spoke. "Now, now, Vance. There's no need to say more. The Spook will have to be replaced, won't he Bill?"

I looked at both of them for a long time, knowing the distinguished Spook could never be replaced. Bob gave me a look of agitation and I finally muttered something to the effect of, "Yah, sure he will."

Marlow glimmered at my words. "Then the matter is as good as settled, gentlemen. I wouldn't be remorseful if I were you. After all, when an old horse wears out, a farmer simply purchases a new one. Good luck then gentlemen, and good day."

What a farce. In the first place, we weren't so damn gentlemanly as he kept repeating, and in the second place, I never thought we bought drivers. Oh sure, we paid them plenty, but the spirit had always existed that we were a team, fighting to win with a product we had faith and believed in, but after that... Besides, how could that fat-assed yes man compare a damn plow horse to a driver on the circuit? Not just any driver at that, but him, the Spook.

I looked Bob squarely in the eye and he couldn't match my gaze, but dropped his eyes and left for the din of the shop, where the team's engines were turning up at high revs. Maybe the noise of the 501's would ease his conscience, but their banshee voices only tended to remind me more of him, who was their fatigued master. A weight pressing on my shoulders, I stepped slowly through the office, the showroom and finally the street itself. Climbing into the company Dodge, I headed for the Spook's motel, to inform him of his betrayal, that I had been unwillingly but nonetheless a part of.

Yes, the word was out; death to the driving force, death to the Spook.

If only I had known then the full meaning of what my wandering thoughts suggested!

The Spook had bought a new Plymouth Fury through Bob and it was the fast, sleek machine that he was tinkering with when I arrived.

"Hello Bill," he greeted, his face haggard and thin.

"Hi Spook," I answered, feeling dirty and clammy with my information.

"Have you any idea why I'm here Spook?"

"Sure Bill, I saw Vance Marlow sniffing around town today."

"It's worse than you surmise, I'm afraid Spook." I shuddered under the full smothering blow of the terrible eyes as they measured me in silent speculation, when I told him of the meeting and it's decisive though unjust outcome.

"You know that you could drive for me any time if I had a voice in it, but as it is, I…" My words were going unheard, as he turned and caressed the glittering hook of the Fury, saying, "too late….too late."

What was too late and what the hell was wrong in the first place? These and numerous other questions raced through my mind, concerning that strange man, but I knew it would do no good to ask him for I had already been politely dismissed. Shrugging, I stepped into the Dodge, swung around and headed back for the shop, thoroughly disgusted with myself and those responsible for their faithlessness and disloyalty.

Driving along, my mind in a fog, I passed Barney's station. I jabbed the brakes, bringing the Dodge to a screeching halt and crammed the shifting lever in reverse. I should have returned to the shop, but the damnabel gall taste in my mouth would not go away.

Barney always kept a fresh fifth or two in his lube room and I thought maybe the sharp bite of alcohol would wash some of the shame I felt away. As for the shop, the damned customers could wait.

"Ah Billy me bye….and what bring ye to me humble establishment this fine day?"

I told that old black Irisher how I felt, explaining the dismissal of the Spook.

With a sly glint to his sky blue eyes, he waved me to his cluttered office in the lube room, while brother Mike held the fort down out front.

"Tis with a grieving heart I receive your news, Billy. Not so much for Spook, as for you and Bob. You know that he'll be out to win on his own, and pity those that gets in his way Billy, pity them." Barney stated emotionally, continuing. "Tis the lone wolf's blood that flows in his pale veins, Billy Boy. He's that rare breed who needs absolutely no one, no one at all."

Maybe old Barney was convinced himself, but then, he hadn't seen what peace the glowing, green eyes could give the Spook. He needed those eyes like the parched earth needs the rains.

"They be a self-reliant breed Billy, with not a feelin for the likes of you and me. Mark me words Billy, I'm sayin the circuit will be hearin from the pale youngster before long."

As old Barney's words echoed in my ears and the warm drink slipped down my throat, the unmistakable sound of a high winding engine and precision up shifts filled the disheveled office. Barney and I ran out front in time to see a Plymouth Fury shifted to third gear at 80 miles per, and go darting for the old Colton River highway. I made a mental note to have Elmer substitute another number for the Spook's previous mount, as it looked as though a number 30 Fury was forthcoming.

"Yonder goes your Spook Billy, yonder goes your Spook."

Yes, yonder went my Spook, and I could picture the man at the wheel of the white and gold Fury, his soul afire once more, the terrible eyes and the face, a driving force...

For several weeks we saw nothing of him. Barney said he had seen Doc Toner at the Spook's motel at different times, and said also that there was much activity in an old deserted garage behind the motel.

I wondered about Doc's business with the Spook, but the thought was lost in the excitement of assuming that he would soon be back on the circuit. If only he could take it a little easy.

Buck had taken the Spook's place to a certain degree, and lead the team very impressively, suffering but one major defeat at the hands of the Keikhafer 300-B's, out of six events.

The Ford Interceptors were constantly crowding us, and on a sultry afternoon in August, Curtis Turner and Fireball Roberts of the Ford factory, made it a one, two finish for their side.

Buck's 501 had been wrecked in the twentieth lap on the Polson road course, and Jerry suffered fuel line clogging, Pat simply couldn't escape the aggressive duo and their fine performing Interceptors, finishing in fifth position one lap behind Turner and Roberts.

After waiting in expectation for a few days, no rebuffs were thrown at us from either Vance Marlow, or the Dodge factory.

Mary, informed of the Spook's intentions was present at all the contests, anxiously watching for any sign of him. Whenever a Fury was anywhere near the course, she would gape at the sleek, scintillating superstock until it was driven away, or Marty, whose hand she usually held, gently told her "no Mary, it isn't him." She suffered much anxiety, but was finally rewarded for her vigilance, later in that same month.

The cars had already begun time trials, all attention focused on the powerful "stock cars". Mary and Marty were watching Buck post what was to be fast time of the event, when Marty said, "Mary!" Her tone of voice was taut and nervous.

The number 30 excelled in sparkling magnitude only by the gold streak on the side of the Fury, stood out boldly and defiantly as the car skipped gingerly into position for trials.

A decrepit, old Dodge pickup, loaded down with spare wheels and tools, pulled into a pit near ours. Two youth, evidently his pit crew began unloading the dilapidated truck.

As the Fury catapulted away onto the course, the crowd cheered in approval, as they recognized the flashing, legendary number.

Other than the Spook, the only independent entries were two of Karl Keidhafer's big 3-B's. Of the twenty-five additional, factory backed contestants, Ford represented by two teams of three cars each, as was Chevy. We had our three 501's while Lew Davis from Polson had two 500's. Plymouth was present with a three car team of Fury's, and the Olds manufacturers sponsored five Super Rockets.

The Spook stole the lead from Buck on the first lap, hurtling the Fury through the turns with the magnificence that he had always shown. He proved himself as the uttermost at midpoint of the race, having lapped the entire field, even the snarling 300-B's.

Rudy Lock, somewhat mellowed those past weeks, put his Super Rocket in the slipstream of the Fury, following the gold car at closing distance for several corners. Somehow or other, he jockeyed the yellow Olds to an abreast position with the Fury and screaming into a tight right hand bend at 80 MPH, the rear end of the Olds bumped the side of the Fury. I'm not sure if Rudy was trying to wreck the Spook, but it appeared as though he was going to!

With the greatest of skill, that slender, ashen figure corrected the disastrous sideways slide of the 30 car, and bashed Rudy's Olds in the rear upon straightening out. The yellow 61 car, its coarse pilot not near as proficient as the Spook, did a complete spin on the asphalt, then left the road, plunging down a steep embankment end over end! Rudy had displayed his rancor for the last time!

The Olds had been completely destroyed, burning before the track officials could get to it. Although the strident; Rudy wasn't killed, his life hung in the balance for weeks, and as it worked out, he was a cripple for the remainder of his life, never again touching the controls of a racer.

In the following 3 road races, the Fury swept the field, tempting death at every bend and serpentine, and thwarting the black, bony hand that surely must have been reaching out for its forlorn master, him, the Spook.

He had conversation for no one, not even Miss Mary.

She looked over at him on his completion of a terrific contest, and for the first time, the glowing, green eyes failed to soften the driving force. Mary had lost his devotion, it seemed, and once more he existed only for speed and risk, his heart beats matching each throb of the violent heart of his golden car.

— — — — — — — — — — —

At the conclusion of the next following race he slithered out the window of the bolted closed door and stood staring over at us. At least I thought it was us he was looking at, but upon waving I received no response.

Mary watched him, listening to what the terrible eyes were saying. She suddenly gasped and ran to him. He opened his arms to her and they embraced for an eternity. He kissed her forehead, her nose and cheeks. He kissed her mouth and finally the shining eyes themselves. Mary's pallor matched his own and they were one weeping openly and unashamed. In both their eyes was something I had never seen before. Was it fear? Marty and I watch hypnotized, not feeling one bit guilty because they had grown on us and what happened between them somehow affected our own lives. Marty looked at me and I think it was fear showing in her face. Her words of only a short time ago came back to me; "Something terrible is going to happen Bill, and Mary will be hurt. It's him Bill, can't you see...?"

Yes, I could always see, I think but how does one cope with such a situation? Mary came toward us as if in a trance, the vibrant, green eyes were saying, and the pain and despair in them was an awful thing to see. What had the terrible eyes of him, the Spook, told her? Something formidable was in the atmosphere about us and I was afraid.

Everything happened so swiftly. Suddenly the cars were in position for the main event, the crowd's yelling and whistling lost in the din of the super-cars, then they were away, the 30 car guided by the cold hand of him, was thrown into the turns even faster than it was accustomed to! The horrible fire that drove him was raging beyond control....

Nordic had no intentions of stopping the race, Doc thought. He must have been a part of the plot to destroy "the boys". Yes, that was it, Doc was sure as he picked up a huge sledge hammer and ran screaming onto the track.

"I'll stop you, you hideous devils. I'll stop you!"

A golden car came sliding out of the north turn, accelerating down the long straightaway In a semi-conscious condition from lack of sleep, the Spook corrected for the rear wheel drift of the golden Fury, mumbling incoherently, as if actually conversing with that machine, which displayed a champion's heart. Well, it was nearly over. Surely, there wasn't much time left for him, Doc had said as much. Why not quit now he thought. He could be in Mary's arms for a little while anyway, before the bugs gobbled all his life's blood up.

That's what to do. He spoke loud to the charging Fury; "One more lap, my little beauty, and we rest. Let's make it the fastest lap ever turned". His glassy eyes cleared some as he was nearly opposite the pits, travelling at 160 MPH!

That's when the hunched-over shape of a man, a sledge hammer in his grasp darted in front of the golden car screaming like one demented!

His instant reflexes automatically made him twist the steering wheel of the 30 car to avoid the fool in his path.

The Fury, accustomed to obeying the master's magic hands without question shuddered at this disastrous request, but nevertheless, obeyed its master. The Fury went out of control, sideways for a split second, then lost its footing altogether!

The Spook, through eyes suddenly gone clear and free from the terrible fire, saw that the red flag was out as the shuddering Fury rolled over and over....

He was killed instantly! I couldn't grasp it. I wanted to yell, scream, or anything, but I couldn't move. If only... I buried my face in my arms. Indeed...it had been too late.

She was there at the funeral, white and pale like the one she loved so deeply. The glowing, green eyes were no more. That was the last time we ever saw her…and sometimes I wake up nights wondering, could she be with him? Wouldn't he have come for her?

What are the earthly limitations that we are all bound by? Surely, with a love as great and intense as was theirs…it could only be right that they were together…somewhere.

I still sell Dodges for Bob, but never get down to the circuit anymore. I don't know…the spirit seems to be gone out of things for me. Yes, maybe that's it…THE SPIRIT is gone!

— — — — — — — — — — —

It is interesting to note, that at the end of the 1956 racing season, Karl Keikhaefer withdrew his dominant Chrysler 300's from further competition…

He had proven all that he had set out to accomplish, and when he had left, he stated: "they copied all they could copy- but they couldn't copy my mind- so I left em sweatin and stealin- a year and a half behind."

This then was Karl Keikhafer - Author

CPSIA information can be obtained at www.ICGtesting.com
Printed in the USA
BVOW03*1649210514

354101BV00012B/343/P